The
Good Son

The
Good Son

Russel D. McLean

Minotaur Books   New York

To Mum and Dad
With huge amounts of love.
But, sadly, still not enough money
to buy that house in France.

A THOMAS DUNNE BOOK FOR MINOTAUR BOOKS.
An imprint of St. Martin's Publishing Group

THE GOOD SON. Copyright © 2008 by Russel D.
McLean. All rights reserved. Printed in the United
States of America. For information, address St.
Martin's Press, 175 Fifth Avenue, New York, N.Y.
10010.

www.thomasdunnebooks.com
www.minotaurbooks.com

Library of Congress Cataloging-in-Publication Data

McLean, Russel D.
    The good son / Russel D. McLean. — 1st U.S. ed.
        p. cm.
    ISBN 978-0-312-57668-4
    1. Private investigators—Fiction.   2. Scotland—
Fiction.   I. Title.
    PR6113.C545G66 2009
    823'.91—dc22   2009028711

First published in Great Britain by Five Leaves
Publications

10 9 8 7 6 5 4 3 2

I could kill him.

It would be easy.

I'm pointing this gun right between his eyes and he looks like he's laughing at the best joke he ever heard.

The only thing that keeps him going is the thought that I won't pull the trigger. He said it himself: I don't have the balls.

Prove him wrong.

Pull the trigger.

It's no less than he deserves.

I've already shot a man this evening, so what's the difference now? Like smoking, it gets easier after the first one, right?

The image is still clear in my brain. The bald bastard, the look of surprise on his face, the way his body stops moving suddenly like he's walked into a wall. The way he just crumples, lands in a heap on the sodden ground.

The rain stings my skin, a thousand pins falling from the sky point first. There's a weight behind them that threatens to push me down into the sod. Root me in the ground like one of these gravestones.

The man in front of me is laughing. Beaten. Battered. But laughing. When he grins I see he's missing a tooth.

My leg buckles.

He sees it, and his grin widens. He thinks he's spotted a weakness.

Not that it matters. Because he'll be dead before he

5

can do anything.

Forget your fucking principles. Think about Kat. The ragged hole in the centre of her forehead.

Her body left in some empty shitehole of a flat.

Broken.

Violated.

Think about Daniel Robertson. Hanging by the neck. Only realising what a mess he made of his life as he struggled to take that final breath.

I hear voices nearby.

The police.

The fucking cavalry.

Which means it's now or never.

No more thinking.

Just act.

Kill the prick.

Think about the people who'll never know justice.

Bill, who might never walk again.

Elaine.

Jesus Christ, Elaine.

I've been looking for someone to blame. And who gives a crap that this isn't the guy?

Might as well be.

Might as well be every prick who ever took a human life.

Might as well be every messed-up fuckbag who killed for kicks or got his fucking rocks off watching his victims plead for mercy.

And that's why I should do this.

That's why this bastard should die.

Chapter 1

Nearly a week before the night I found myself ready to kill a man in cold blood, I was angling for the security of a job that paid up front.

Which is why I was grateful for the business of any client. Especially the man who huffed his way into the offices of McNee Investigations.

James Robertson stuffed himself into the sixties-style recliner I'd picked up a few weeks earlier at the Salvation Army store on West Marketgait. He was sweating, even though it was a cool day. As if he'd swum across the Tay rather than taking the bridge. The handkerchief tucked into the breast pocket of his suit jacket looked damp.

I offered my hand. His was slick and threatened to slip from my grasp.

It wasn't his size, even if he was a large man. No, the sweat came from agitation. Robertson was tense, his muscles practically humming they were stretched so taut.

After I introduced myself, he bobbed his head up

7

and down as though agreeing with me. "It's a climb up those stairs, Mr McNee," he said, a strong Fife accent making him sound accusatory. His little eyes regarded me suspiciously. "For a man like myself, of course." His features crumpled in thought. "McNee," chewing the name over. He smiled. "Like the actor!" I shrugged the observation off, having heard it a hundred times before. "You're younger than I would have thought."

Did he mean this merely as an observation or as something more subtly insulting? I let it go, and showed him into my private office. He followed, even though he seemed reluctant to leave the recliner.

Robertson looked around the private room, nodded approvingly at the minimalist decoration.

"Are you okay?" he asked. Hadn't taken him long to notice.

I shook my head.

"Bad looking limp."

Not so bad. Not now. Could have been worse.

I could have lost my life.

"Doesn't interfere with the job, Mr Robertson, if that's what you're worried about."

He shook his head like the thought had never crossed his mind.

Aye, right.

I gestured for him to sit down. He took one of the padded chairs in front of my desk. I stayed standing, asked him why he was here.

"The other fellow," he said. "The one who used to work here. He had a reputation, you know?"

I nodded. "Sure. You knew him?"

"Not personally. He did work for some... people I know."

I didn't ask what kind of work or what kind of

people. That would have been unprofessional.

The other investigator had been in business at least a decade, using these same offices. The centre of Dundee. Prime location. Down the road from the Sheriff's Court, too. It wasn't just the location, of course, that had helped build him a local reputation.

I met him before I took over the property, thought he looked old before his time. He said, that's what the business does to you. The implication was clear: I wouldn't keep my fresh-faced looks for too long.

Then again, maybe I'd keep them longer than he expected.

"I can give you references," I said. "I used to be a copper."

"Aye?" Robertson took out his handkerchief, wiped his forehead. "Surely that's a wee bit more respectable than all this?" He gestured expansively and then let out a sigh.

I wondered, did he mean the office or the lifestyle?

Probably the lifestyle. In the UK, the life of an investigator is hardly seen as glamorous. We don't have the same lone-wolf mythology as our counterparts in the US. If people think of us, it's as sleazy, cheap last-resorts. And in Scotland, we're barely even thought of at all.

I waited, watching my client: how he moved, the set of his face, the way his eyes darted about the office. Afraid to settle anywhere, especially on me.

"What can I do for you?" I asked.

"You can tell me about my brother."

I pulled out a tape recorder, placed it on the table. Robertson looked at the device, and then nodded his consent. I wasn't writing anything down. This was a friendly wee chat. Recorded for posterity.

Funny how people open up to a recorder and yet

clam up when they see you scribbling.

"Your brother?" I prompted.

"Do you read the papers?"

"I keep up."

"The *Tele*?" he asked, meaning *The Evening Telegraph*: local paper for local people.

"Sure."

"Then you know my name," he said. "Or you should. Nosy bastards slapped it all over the front page couple of nights ago."

I nodded, then; realised who he was.

"James Robertson," I said, like I'd just heard his name for the first time. "I'm sorry for your loss."

Chapter 2

Like I said, people open up to a recorder. All I had to do to get Robertson's story was prod him once or twice in the right direction. Keep him focused.

The Robertson family farm, he told me, sat out across the bridge near St Michaels; a small hamlet on the outer edges of Tentsmuir Forest. Robertson — out of habit more than anything else — took a quick pint at the local pub most nights.

Two weeks earlier, Robertson had run into the pub. Ready to collapse from a coronary. Not just through exertion, either.

The barman gave Robertson a drink, calmed him down enough for the man to explain what had happened. He described how he'd found a body out in the woods and how the poor bastard swinging from the branch of a long dead tree was his brother, who he hadn't seen for over thirty years.

The police responded within twenty minutes. Two bobbies out of Cupar — the nearest town with a sizeable station — walked into the pub, their swagger of

11

authority tempered by an air of apprehension. They talked to Robertson briefly and he led them to the body.

As one of the policemen moved to investigate the swinging corpse, the other tried to keep Robertson from passing out. The farmer was on his knees, the harsh rasp of his breathing mutating into a deep hyperventilation. The copper tried to persuade the farmer to breathe easier and make him feel like he had a friend. Robertson wasn't alone.

Except he was.

***

"Maybe it's in the genes, aye?"

"What's in the genes?"

Robertson looked at me like I was stupid. "Suicide," he said. "Depression. All that nonsense."

"You've had suicidal tendencies?"

"No, not me!" Agitated, his eyes bugging. "My — our — father."

"Your father killed himself?"

"Rest his soul."

"Why?"

His brow rumpled. "I couldn't tell you for sure."

There was nothing else to say except, "I'm sorry."

"Spare me," he said. "Christ, please, anything but that."

"What I don't understand is why you require the services of an investigator."

"I told you, me and Daniel didn't talk. Not properly. The occasional letter, but even then... Our father had a heart attack a few years back."

"But I thought —"

"He survived. Pulled through. Stubborn man, Dad.

At least he was... after the attack, it just took everything out of him... Makes you wish the heart attack had been fatal." Robertson looked on the verge. Ready to jump. The tears waiting to flow.

But it didn't happen.

Real men — Scots men — don't cry.

I waited as Robertson composed himself.

Finally: "I always thought that would be how he'd go. A heart attack, I mean. Better than suicide, right? I wrote to Daniel and told him. To let him know. That the old man was all right. Got back a one-line letter."

"What did it say?"

He hesitated. Then, whispering the words as though afraid of reprisal: "It said, 'No worse than the old cunt deserves.'"

"How old was your brother when he left?"

"Sixteen. An argument with Dad."

"Where'd he go?"

"Down to England. London."

"I still don't see what..."

"Mr McNee, I don't know what happened to my brother down there. I don't even know what he did for a living. I know nothing about him, the man he became. All I know is that he had a forwarding address. A place I could reach him. That, and two months after our dad dies, I find Danny's corpse swinging from a tree."

I could have forgiven him the tears earlier.

"You want closure."

"The police don't seem to..."

I understood that.

"They're happy to know how. But they don't care why."

"Aye," said Robertson. "Aye, that's the problem."

I sat back in the chair, kept my eyes locked on him.

13

He continued looking down at his belly.

"What I find could be even more upsetting than..."

"Peace of mind," he said. "That's what's important here." There was finality in the statement. An answer to every objection I could raise.

I laid out my fee structure. He listened, nodded, said, "Of course, Mr McNee," pulled out a chequebook from his inside pocket.

***

I looked out the office window onto Ward Road. The DSS office across the way was a foreboding block of dark concrete that edged onto North Lindsay Street. Robertson walked past the building and down towards the car park at the rear of the new Overgate Shopping Centre, part of Dundee's recent rejuvenation. Sandstone from the rear, glass and steel from the front. The gently curving structure hooked round the City Churches and St Mary's Steeple like the protective arm of a mother round the shoulders of a child.

The Centre was a far cry from the decrepit block of 1960's concrete that had preceded it. The mall was just one sign of a city looking to forget its industrial roots and move forward; part of the new, modern Scotland. Forget the tat that feeds the tourist trade: we're out on the cutting edge.

Jam, Jute and Journalism — the heritage of the city every child is taught in school — was history. The Overgate and Riverside Developments were in line with Scotland's new cosmopolitanism. Embracing the modern world. They'd called Dundee the City of Discovery. Not just a reference to Captain Scott's ship, permanently anchored down by the Riverside.

Scientific and medical research had been pumping cash into Dundee since the late nineties. Computer programmers had found their Mecca — *Grand Theft Auto* was created here. An unexpected financial boon for the city so many Scots had been ready to write off.

Bill, whose official title is administrative assistant, smiled as I walked into reception. "That looked like a man with problems."

I nodded.

Bill smoothed his hair down with an unnecessary gesture. He took great stock in his appearance, each item of clothing chosen carefully. Never a crease. His hair was held in place by so many products you could have set him alight by flicking a lighter under his nose. But his voice was what defied expectations. It was down in his boots; a gravelly native rumble that could stop a bar brawl.

I took his copy of the previous evening's *Tele* off the desk, checked the by-line on the lead story.

Daniel Robertson's suicide still dominated the local news, but the tone of the article made it clear that the police had come to the end of their inquiries. It had become a non-story. To everyone except the dead man's brother.

***

Much of an investigator's work these days is sedentary. Technology has made it a static job. The bread-and-butter work doesn't involve much action. You sit at a desk, you check files. You wait for hours in the driver's seat of a car for just the right moment, your camera ready to capture the evidence.

Sometimes you get out. Photograph accident sites

for insurance claims. Talk to people. Try and get information. But much of that can be done over the phone just as easily as in person.

I started locally.

Called the Fife constabulary media inquiries office.

"How can I help?"

I glanced at the *Tele,* used the name of the reporter whose name appeared on the Robertson story. "My name's Cameron Connelly. I'm calling regarding the suicide of Daniel Robertson." For a moment, I worried the woman on the other end might know Connelly, realise I was pulling a fast one. Relying on the fact they were across the other side of the river. Fife Constabulary wouldn't deal so much with Dundonian journalists. I was taking a gamble.

Either I was right, or the girl on the other end was new, hadn't played the *getting to know you* game with the local hacks. "Haven't you got anything better to write about?"

I almost sighed with relief.

Instead, I said, "Slow news week."

"Must be."

"I heard a rumour today…"

"You should know better…"

"There's more to this man's death than the police are telling us." There always is. The police and the media play an odd game of cat and mouse as reporters fight for more information and the coppers try to hold it back.

The woman on the other end of the line paused. Just a little too long. Then: "It was a suicide. The coroner confirmed it. I don't know what else you want, Mr Connelly."

"No evidence of foul play?"

She laughed. "Really scraping the barrel over

16

there, aren't you?"

"Guess so," I said. And hung up.

Confirmation of suicide. But they were holding something back. Didn't want to give it to the press. Check the hesitations and the avoidance strategies.

I didn't have much. But I had a name. And an address.

Could have been worse.

Daniel Robertson's mail was forwarded to a nightclub in the heart of Soho. His brother had been writing to the address for years. A quick search gave me the club's website. Glitzy, expensive, with an overly busy design. It took me a while to find the information I needed.

A name leaped out.

The club's owner.

Gordon Egg.

Even north of the border, I'd heard of him. A new wave London gangster, born too late to have power when the Krays ruled the underworld, but old enough to have amassed a reputation and even make a late grab at respectability.

His book — he called it *Hard Boiled*, the best kind of double pun — had hit the shelves two years earlier. It played on his violent past, appealing to a market that didn't want to read, but idolised men like Egg.

The website didn't disguise the facts. Instead it played them up. Made a big deal about the business being run by an "ex" East End gangster. A wide boy made good.

I thought: men like that don't go straight.

If Daniel was involved with Egg, maybe his brother wouldn't want to know the truth.

I'd already said I wasn't going to lie. And Robertson had claimed he was ready to accept whatever I told him.

I grabbed the phone, rang the club. It was still early, but there was every chance someone would be around, getting the place ready for the evening. A caretaker, at least, who might know something.

A rough East End voice answered the phone.

"I'm looking for Daniel Robertson," I said.

A pause.

"He don't work here no more."

"It's important. I'm calling on behalf of his family."

"Gotcha," said the voice. "Thought you sounded fuckin' Scotch, mate. But all the same, he ain't workin' here no more. Got his arse fired, didn't he?"

"When did that happen?"

The guy on the other end hesitated before saying "Three weeks ago."

"No wonder we can't get hold of him."

"He said he wasn't that close to his family."

"What did he do? I mean, that he got fired?"

"Confidential information, that is, mate. Don't know you from Adam. Could be anyone callin' us, asking for info on someone's done something you don't like."

"Aye, of course." Keeping my voice breezy. "If you hear from him, tell him his brother wants a word."

"Sure thing." He hung up.

I kept the receiver near my ear for a few moments. Listening to the dial tone. Daniel had been fired from the club three weeks earlier. Whatever happened, his departure hadn't been under the best of circumstances. A bite to the Cockney's voice told me his opinion of Daniel Robertson. More than just antagonism towards the Scots.

I placed the receiver back in the cradle, stood up and hit the kettle that sat on top of a four-drawer

18

filing cabinet.

Thought about Daniel Robertson. Tried to find a point of connection.

Who had he become?

If the company he kept was any indication, he hadn't found the streets of London paved with gold.

There was a guy I used to know on the force who'd transferred down south to the Met. We said we'd keep in touch, but that was never one of my strong points. We hadn't talked in three years.

Last I knew he'd been working with the drugs squad. I called around, asked questions, waited on extensions until finally I reached the man himself.

His voice had become corrupted by an encroaching English twang. The mixed accent sounded artificial and unpleasant. He used my first name.

I winced.

"Dave," I said. "How are you?"

"Jesus, mate, haven't heard from you in donkeys..."

"Tell me about it."

"You still in Dundee?"

"Aye."

"Christ, you should have transferred out while you could. That prick Lindsay still about?"

"Oh, yeah."

"You mean you haven't tried to kill him?"

"They don't look kindly on murdering a superior officer."

"Guess not." He sounded happy to hear from me. And evidently still believed I was on the force. Which also meant he wouldn't know about...

"How's Elaine?"

Last time we spoke, we'd been down the pub. Drinking his health, wishing him luck.

Elaine had kissed his cheek.

I pictured the scene.

Held it.

Said, "She's dead."

Sounding flat and emotionless.

Must have knocked Dave on his arse. He went quiet enough.

The phone went off in reception.

"Jesus, mate, I'm sorry." He sounded hollow. False. But then so did everyone when they told me that, and I had to wonder whether it was more me than him.

"It's fine. Been nearly nine months, now. Accident. Some prick ran her car off the road."

"They ever catch him?"

"Like on *Taggart*?"

He took the admonishment surprisingly well. "Got to be hard on you."

"I'm surviving." I switched the subject. No subtlety involved. No need. What else did he have to know? "I'm calling to ask a favour. I know it's been a while, but..."

"What do you need?"

"It's a case I'm working on... just background shit, really... we have a suicide here. Came up from London, and I think he might have been involved in a few dodgy dealings on your patch."

"He have a name, this suicide?"

"Daniel Robertson."

"I'll see what I can find. That all you called for?"

"I'm sorry," I said. "You were the best contact I could..."

"Contact," he said, and didn't even bother to hide any bitterness. "We were friends, yeah?"

"This was kind of urgent. I..."

"Nah, leave it with me. I'll get back to you." His voice light again, but it was an affectation, maybe thinking he didn't want to upset the poor bereaved fuck on the other end of the line.

"Thanks."

"One colleague to another, yeah?"

"Sure."

I gave him my number and he hung up without saying goodbye. Taking it personally, the fact that I only called after so long to discuss a case. Maybe he was right. We'd been good friends. I'd been an usher at his marriage to a girl called Jennifer. Pretty young Irish lass with short, blonde hair and blue eyes that sparkled with a maliciously good-natured wit.

After the marriage, Dave and his wife moved down south. There were promises made about keeping in touch.

I thought about Elaine telling me that I wouldn't have any friends if I didn't work with them, and even then I was never really one of the lads, was I? She had me pegged. Every fault and every insanity. And still she acted like she loved me.

For that I was always grateful.

There was a knock at the door. I looked up to see Bill pop his head through. John-Lennon-style reading glasses sat halfway down his nose, and he peered at me over the top of the frames like a stern English teacher. "You okay, boss?"

"Aye, sure. I'd forgotten how knackering it was making phone calls."

He bought it, or at least bulldozed past the subject. "There was a phone call while you were on the other line. Bloody odd. Some woman. Sounded like a Londoner, could have been auditioning for EastEnders. Calls up, asks what we want with 'Danny'."

21

That got my attention. "Danny?"

"Aye. I said I couldn't help her, but I remembered the name of that suicide…"

"Daniel Robertson."

"Yeah, that's him… but he's dead… And why would we —?"

"I don't think everyone knows it, yet. That he's dead."

Bill looked ready to say something. But he stopped himself. Turned his head to the side, licked his lips.

Like he was thinking about something.

Finally: "Making progress?"

"Some."

"You don't hang about."

"Motivated by cash."

"Aren't we all?"

"Did she leave a name and number, this woman?"

"No. She hung up. But I did a 1471."

He passed a scrap of paper. London code. Familiar number. I checked it.

Egg's club.

"Thanks, Bill."

He left without another word. I dialled, got the same gruff Cockney who answered before.

He recognised me, too. "Told you already, mate, Daniel ain't here."

"Someone called me back. Might have been someone who knew Daniel. A woman."

"Nah, mate, nobody's called you back. No woman here. Not today."

"If there's anyone you can—"

Forcefully, this time: "I'm telling you, it's a fucking mistake."

I pulled the receiver away from my ear, looked at it as though it held all the answers I could ever want.

Chapter 3

I played a game of solitaire while I waited. Relaxing. Distracting.

Aye. Right.

I listened to the answer phone message I'd kept for the past three days.

"McNee, it's Rachel. I know you think you're not welcome here, but... Jesus, he just needs someone to blame. She would have wanted you to come. She would have wanted you to be with us."

Elaine's sister was right. Elaine had always seemed proud that I was accepted by her family. That the man who made no personal connections, had no family of his own, would make an effort to fit in with such a tight knit clan as the Barrows. But I had done it for her, and now that she was gone, I was slipping away from them again.

Exactly what some of them might have wished for.

I turned off the machine.

Massaged my forehead for a moment.

Grabbed the phone when it rang.

"You're a lying prick." It was Dave.

"Sorry?" Playing it innocent.

"You're no longer with the force."

"I wasn't sure that you'd want to share with an investigator. Besides, I didn't lie."

"Just omitted the truth. Sure, mate. Right enough."

"This means you're not going to help me?"

"I'll tell you what I can. Email you the reports. And then I say you're not calling me again. Got it?"

"Sure."

What Dave told me wasn't much. Daniel had been a bouncer at one of Egg's clubs in the 90s. He was close to the man, became head of security when he got older. Because of his criminal record, he failed to get his license when the law changed.

I asked, "What kind of record?"

"Violent. ABH, GBH, the usual suspects." He was quiet for a moment. "Tell me why you need to know again?"

"He left behind family. Family who didn't know him."

"They don't want to."

"Not my decision."

"I like it," said Dave, his voice flat. "Lack of responsibility. Confirms everything I ever thought about your lot."

I was the enemy, now. No longer even an ex-friend, I had become the force's antagonist. The guy who stepped on their toes, who fucked them over. A simple thing that changed relationships I thought I could rely on. The real reason I'd failed to mention my new profession when we talked earlier.

"Think that if you like," I said.

"Our friend Danny Robertson was top of the watch

list," said Dave. "A heavy hitter. If you've got any sense left, you'll stay clear of this shit. Tell your client you pass on his generous payment and take on someone else's misery."

"I'll take that under advisement."

"I should go," said Dave. "Got some real work to take care of."

"Yeah," I said. "Give Jen my best."

"We're separated."

Five minutes earlier I might have said I was sorry. Maybe even meant it. I cleared the line before he beat me to it.

***

The header of Dave's email: "Now fuck off."

Cute.

Attached were arrest reports and photographs.

I read the reports.

Didn't even notice Bill leaving for the evening.

My eyes strained.

I went through to reception, walked around a bit waiting for the kettle to boil. Sat on the recliner Robertson had used. Closed my eyes for just a moment.

***

It wasn't the usual nightmare. I was grateful for that until I realised I was standing in the city centre, outside *Fat Sam's* nightclub.

The sky was a dark grey, lost somewhere between evening and night. I couldn't see a sun or a moon. The streetlights were off, but it was bright enough to see.

People queued up outside the club. I stood where I was, just scanning the faces. They were blurred, unreal.

Jesus, not like real people queued up to get into the clubs anyway.

What I couldn't figure was why so many of the voices that drifted across the street to me in garbled fragments sounded like Cockney hard men. No local accents at all. As if the whole scene had been displaced.

My eyes moved to the front of the queue.

I didn't recognise any of the bouncers.

Until one of them looked directly at me.

The eyes caught my attention first. Grey, intense. Below a heavy brow on a face lined with anger.

His body had developed in direct contrast to his brother's. Daniel Robertson was lean, not an ounce of fat on him. His stance was confrontational; a soldier in the middle of a combat zone.

I looked away.

He saw it, recognised fear.

And he was standing over me. Crossing the space between us without appearing to have moved at all. I could hear him breathing.

Slow.

Heavy.

Intense.

He said, "Your name's not down."

I backed away.

Into a wall.

The crowds were gone. Now the club was closed up and it was just the two of us standing on the street.

Looking past him, it wasn't even Fat Sam's any more. It was another club, one I'd never seen before. I noted the name above the door.

Egg's.

"You think he'd let a prick like you inside?"

"I don't want in."

"Then what do you want?"

I couldn't say.

"Then what do you want?" he repeated.

He was a giant, now, looming above me, his features hidden by shadow. The world around us had turned black and the only other sound was the pumping music that came from the club.

I wanted to fight back. But I was no longer in control of my own body.

"If you don't know what you want, what are you doing here?"

All I could see now was his fist. I could count the hairs on the backs of his knuckles.

My stomach jumped not only with fear but with another strange sensation. A mix of loss and guilt that made me feel as though I was about to explode.

I closed my eyes.

Waited.

And then the sky was bright, once more. And someone was standing over me. He smirked when he saw me. His nose was recently broken, pressed flat against the rest of his face. It might have been comical if I hadn't known him.

He shook his head, like he was disappointed with me.

"Really," said DI George Lindsay. "Just stay away from that prick. Unless you want to get yourself killed."

***

I forced my eyes open, found I was sitting in the recliner. My leg protested. I made a low groaning

27

noise as I stood up. My arms were heavy and useless and my vision was still blurred with sleep.

I felt restless, as though there was something else I should have been doing.

The phone screamed.

I stumbled into my office, noticed the black skies outside the window, didn't even think to look at the time.

"McNee Investigations."

"You called the club."

"I did."

"What do you want with Danny?" The voice was female, somewhere in her early fifties, perhaps. She croaked from years of cigarettes and alcohol. Boozy, broken, oddly fragile. Made me think of Marianne Faithfull.

"Who are you?"

"I knew him."

"How well?"

"Jesus fuck! You're a nosy bastard."

"It's my job."

"Yeah?"

"I'm an investigator."

"'Course, yeah."

"I'm working for his family."

"All his family's down here..."

"His brother."

"Bloody hell, those two don't even —"

"There's something I need to talk to you—"

I heard other noises in the background.

"Fuck! I need to go. Jesus, but you're right, yeah? We need to—"

The line went dead.

I hoped it was just the line.

Chapter 4

I woke up around six the next morning. Stretched, working out the kinks in my muscles. Fell to the floor and straight into a sequence of push ups before rolling over and crunching the stomach muscles.

My leg ached with the exertions. I did my best to ignore it.

According to the doctors at Ninewells, I shouldn't be feeling any pain. I should be céilidh dancing without breaking a sweat. But what did they know?

They'd told me to throw away the crutches months ago. I never did. They were still back at my flat. Because no matter what the doctors said, I knew my leg was fucked for life.

Another hour before Bill started work.

I cleaned up, made it look like I'd arrived early. I didn't want him to think I'd been here all night.

I felt more comfortable staying at the office than my own place.

Maybe that made sense. I still lived in the flat I had shared with Elaine. At nights, when I sat on the sofa and let my mind relax, I thought I could see her sitting across from me with her legs curled up and a book in her hands.

She was still there in my bed. I would awake at night and feel the heat from her body.

I had been offered the chance to join support groups after her death. Even though I had refused at the time, I still wondered whether what I experienced was only a natural part of the grieving process. A refusal to admit she was gone.

It seemed better — healthier even — to remain at the office and throw myself into a world where I could escape her memory. At least for a while.

It's an escape tactic that has worked well for the McNees. Certainly for my father, who distracted himself with work rather than face any real emotional issues. It was a side of him that my mother had simply accepted.

There was something of my father in my features. Just a touch.

I wondered what I would look like if I ever stopped moving long enough to truly consider what Elaine's death had meant to me.

Remembered how my father looked before the end. Was that what awaited me?

I smoothed out my hair with my hands and looked closely at myself in the mirror. Somewhere close to human.

I moved through to my office, powered up the computer. Browsed my emails.

Distractions.

***

At half past one, Bill rang through from the front office.

"There's—" he paused —"a woman to see you."

I swallowed the last of my pie, told Bill to send her through.

She tottered into my office, looked around and sniffed, unimpressed. "I've come a long way to see you," she said. Cockney trying to sound educated. Low pitch. Familiar.

"I understand," I said. "Can I get you a drink, Ms...?"

"Kat'll do just now," she said. She didn't answer my other inquiry.

But I knew who she was; recognised the voice. The woman who had called from Egg's club. She looked the part, too: heavy makeup. Perm. Fur coat. I'd guessed her age about right. Looked like she was trying to forget it.

"You came all the way from London?"

"Yeah." Her green eyes dared me to make something of it. "Overnight. Soon as I could make it."

"You knew Daniel?"

"I wouldn't have come all this way if I didn't —" She stopped herself, bowed her head. "We were close." She played with her hair. Self-conscious.

"Did you know he was heading north?"

"No one knew where he'd gone."

"No one thought he'd come home?"

"His family," she said. "They hated him." Pronouncing her 'h's with deliberation. "He didn't think much of them, neither." She rubbed the material of her jacket between the thumb and forefinger of her left hand.

"Sure." Digesting what she had to say, watching her reaction. "How did you meet?"

Did I really want to know, or was I just delaying telling her about Daniel's suicide?

31

"What business is it of yours?"

"I'm just curious."

"Why'd you call the club?"

"Part of an investigation."

"What kind of investigation?"

"I can't say."

"Fucking tell me why you called the club." Trying to act tough, but she looked scared. She wouldn't have made the journey if she didn't think something had happened to Daniel.

I thought about the last phone call she'd made. The sound of other voices. The panic when she cleared the line.

She knew Daniel. And the people he worked for.

Over the line, she'd sounded scared. In person, she hid it well. But not well enough.

"I didn't come all the way up to this fucking armpit of an excuse for civilisation to be arsed about by a fucking cunt like you!" Even her anger seemed half-hearted. And I saw it in her eyes; she already knew. She'd guessed. Or she just felt it, somehow.

"Kat," I said. "Daniel's dead."

I could have stabbed her instead. It would have been more merciful.

She let go of her coat. Her mouth slackened. Her petite shoulders jerked up and down. Once. Twice.

"I'm sorry," I said. At least the third time in the last two days...

She bowed her head. A noise escaped her lips. Hesitant. High-pitched and keening.

I kept my distance, wanting to reach out. But I didn't.

Would she even want me to?

She had been standing all this time. I hadn't even

thought to offer her a seat, but now she slumped into the chair on the far side of the desk, hid her face from me with her hands.

Finally, she stopped crying, looked up and said, "They catch who done it?"

I hesitated.

"They even know who done it?"

Not even questioning whether his death was accidental or from natural causes. "Yes," I said. "They know."

"Tell me who."

I told her.

She was on her feet fast, slapping me across the face. "Fuck you," she said. "He'd never do that." She slapped me again. "Fuck you."

I took it. Each blow stung, but I refused to react. Absorbing her anger and pain. A human punching bag.

When she was finished, her green eyes locked onto mine. But the challenge there was non-committal, and she looked away and down at her feet.

"His brother found him," I said. "Not the kind of reunion anyone would welcome. He came to me, asked for my help."

"What could you do?"

"Find out who his brother had become. Tell him what had happened to Daniel in the three decades since they last spoke."

"Daniel wrote him all the time."

"You ever read the letters?"

"No. They were private."

"Sure. But it wouldn't have mattered if you did. He told his brother nothing. Two or three lines. A little less than you get on a postcard."

"They weren't a close family."

33

I didn't know what to say to that. From Daniel's point of view, I guess they weren't. But Robertson talked like family was all that had ever really mattered to him.

"Maybe not, but Daniel's suicide would have opened up a lot of old wounds."

"I get that," she said. She moved to a chair, sat down. "The coppers just ignored it?"

"It was a suicide," I said. "Nothing suspicious. Just the question of why. Not something they seem too interested in answering."

"Just another body."

I hadn't seen the pictures, but in my mind I could see Daniel Robertson with his eyes wide, his mouth open as though he were screaming.

"It's the way they have to look at it," I said.

"Funny thing," she said. "I met you on the street, I'd take you for a copper."

"I used to be one."

"Oh?"

"I walked out."

"You walked or they pushed you?"

I didn't answer.

"If you just walked, then you're a fuckin' wimp." She smiled, then, and said, "That was rude, Mr McNee. I'm sorry. It's just..."

"I understand." But I wanted to tell her I had my reasons.

"You said his brother was the one what found him? You think maybe I could talk to him?"

"If you give me a contact number I'll have him call you."

"Leave it to his discretion?"

"Something like that."

I passed her a pen and a piece of paper. She wrote

down a mobile number. Her script was deliberate, the numbers large and bold. "I'll be in town a little while. I guess I need to do my grieving is all."

"If you need anything..."

She pulled a hankie from her handbag and dabbed delicately at her eyes. The white tissue came away smudged with the black of her mascara.

Chapter 5

"She knew my brother?"

"Aye." I was walking west along Ward Road. Holding the phone tight against my ear as I strained to hear Robertson's voice. "Says she did, anyway."

"Christ," he said. "A wife?"

"Girlfriend," I said. Except she wasn't much of a girl any more. Fake fur and thick makeup hiding the mature woman underneath. It should have been repulsive. Instead, I felt sorry for her.

"How long...?"

"She didn't tell me much. Insisted she'd only speak to you. I told her I couldn't make that decision on your behalf."

Silence on the other end of the line, except for the sound of his breathing.

"If you want my opinion," I said, "I don't think it's a good idea. Give me some time to feel around. I can find out if she's genuine."

"Why would she lie about knowing Daniel?"

"I don't know." A half truth, but I didn't want to

burden him with details of his brother's life over a phone line. A cold way to conduct such personal business.

"Has she given you any reason not to trust her?"

"She hasn't given me a reason to trust her."

"Give me the number."

I stressed again that I didn't think this was a good idea. "Mr Robertson, the facts of your brother's life are... unpleasant."

"Unpleasant?" I could picture his already red face turning a deeper shade of scarlet, the fat of his forehead crinkling around his little eyes.

"I hoped we might discuss this in person."

"This woman — his girlfriend, bidey-in or whatever she is — she's the last link to my brother. If anyone can tell me who he was, then it's her."

He was right. She was tangible. Our last link to Daniel Robertson.

"At least let me have another talk with her... I can —"

"No," he said.

"Then I should be present, at least —"

"I don't think so. This is something I have to do for myself."

There was no talking him out of it.

**

By the time I walked up the two flights to my office, I'd reluctantly given Robertson Kat's number and ended the call. He was my client. I wanted to serve his best interests, but it was hard when he failed to appreciate my efforts.

He didn't really want an investigator. He wanted someone who would reassure him that his brother's life had been peaches and cream and what happened out in the woods was an aberration, perhaps even some perversely heroic gesture.

That was why he wanted to talk to this woman. Maybe she would colour the story just right. Make everything seem perfect. Make Daniel's life more palatable.

Maybe she would lie.

Bill updated me on admin. He mentioned that he would be leaving early. It was his boyfriend's birthday and he'd booked an early meal at a restaurant on Brook Street.

I asked him to pass on my best to Andy and locked myself in my office. Tried not to think about birthdays. Or the message on the answerphone.

I spent the afternoon working on what little I knew about Daniel Robertson. Doing my best not to be judgemental but finding it hard to remain distanced.

The truth: Daniel Robertson was a violent, self-serving bastard with little or no redeeming qualities.

I couldn't sugar coat this. And neither could I afford to shake my client's fragile delusion that his brother had merely been a victim of circumstance.

About nine o'clock, after Bill had left the office, my mobile rang. I answered quickly, not recognising the number.

"I'm down on the street. The lights are on. I guess somebody's home." A Dundonian accent, thick with unrestrained contempt.

I'd been hoping I wouldn't have to hear those dulcet tones again. But in a city the size of Dundee you can't avoid anyone forever.

"You and me, we need to talk."

Like fuck we did. Dreaming about him had been

bad enough.

All the same, I went down to street level, and let him in. He followed me up the stairs in silence.

In the front office, I didn't bother offering him a seat. Just stood there and waited for him to say his piece.

His muscles were tense, as though he was ready to run at a moment's notice. I couldn't blame him. Last time we'd been this close, I'd clocked him one. Broke his nose. Almost nine months later and it was still misshapen.

The slightly bulbous bridge of his nose aside, he looked exactly as I remembered. He stood with his head slightly forward, his shoulders curved. His dark hair was cropped short and his suspicious eyes stared out from below his jutting forehead.

If it weren't for the suit, he would be proof, if any were needed, of Cro-Magnon man's existence in the world today.

"I got a call," he said. "From an inspector working out of Cupar. He wanted to know why some arsehole is calling his station, pretending to be from the local paper."

I folded my arms, straightened my back. "Nice to know."

"Don't fuck me about."

I kept quiet.

"The call came from this number."

"Seems an awful waste of resources, tracing one prank call."

"One prank call that could impede an ongoing investigation."

"Into a suicide?"

That was enough to give him pause. Like he'd given away too much.

He raised his gaze to meet my eyeline as he continued. All confrontation. Giving nothing else away. But it was too late to throw me off the scent. So he went straight for the jugular. "They were, of course, very interested to learn about your, uh, past."

"I'm sure you took a great delight telling them about it."

"Listen to me, you wanker," he said, stepping forward, tilting his head up so I wasn't just looking at the wee bald patch in the centre of his skull. "You were always a trouble maker. Surprised me you stuck things out as long as you did. This investigation crap, it's a game to someone like you."

"Sure, the best games are the ones that leave you worrying how you'll pay the electric bill at the end of the month."

"Always with the fuckin' smart mouth, aye? But this shite is best left to the professionals. You know, the ones the public trust to uphold the bloody law? You think you're some kind of vigilante? Fuck that!"

I stepped back. "You're getting awful worked up over a simple suicide."

"I take my work seriously."

I remembered the satisfaction I felt cracking Lindsay's nose.

Real justice, I remember thinking.

My fingers flexed as I resisted the urge just to smack him one all over again. It wouldn't be worth it. No witnesses and he'd have me hauled down for assaulting an officer of the law.

So instead of fists, I settled for words.

"You just came here to tell me what an arse I am. Face it, Lindsay, you get some kind of fucking perverse pleasure out of hassling me. I dunno, maybe I remind you of the kid who bullied you in school. Aye, the one you've been trying to get back at all your adult life."

"Check out fuckin' McFreud there."

"Get to business or get the fuck out. I'm working."

"Listen to me, you prick. If you're half as good as you think you are, you'll have worked out that our wee dead friend wasn't the nicest of men."

"The police reports say a lot more than that."

"And what the fuck would you know about that?"

I smiled. "Lucky guess."

"You want me to search this place?"

"Go ahead."

He seemed to consider this. I kept myself relaxed.

Finally: "This isn't the kind of thing where you want to be getting in people's way. Let the professionals handle it."

"It wasn't a suicide."

"Don't fuckin' question that, McNee. The daft prick killed himself. No danger." Lindsay stepped back. He pulled a cigarette from his jacket, made to spark up.

I flicked it from his mouth.

"This is a place of business."

He stepped back. His eyes wide. The colour draining from his cheeks. "Aye, sure, for all the work that gets done." He forced a smile. Too late, though, to fool me. "All I'm asking is that you take other people's interests into consideration for once."

"James Robertson came to me. Asked me to look into his brother's life," I said. "He needed closure. Something I could provide. Unlike you lot. You only gave him more grief."

Lindsay's jawline pulsed. That false smile vanished. "Given the sensitivity of —"

I steamrollered over his bullshit. "Which leads me

41

to ask a few questions. Like whether there isn't something else going on here. I know a little about who Daniel became. And you wouldn't be round here beating your chest like an extra in *Planet of the Apes* without a very good fucking reason."

"Has anyone ever told you you're smarter than you look?"

"Daniel was good friends with Gordon Egg. The Met wouldn't just ignore a man that close to the power centre of London's gangland. His suicide's bound to have raised some red flags. They'd have been on the phone to you the minute —"

Lindsay stuck his hands in his pockets and looked at me like he'd found something amusing. "Don't get cocky. Aye, the Met got their knickers in a twist when they found out the bastard was up here. Worse, he'd come back home without them having a bloody clue. Really pissed them off when they realised he'd topped himself."

"He's not the type," I said.

"Right enough, that's what the big brains are saying. Which means you sniffing around like a drug-dog in a crack-house is causing no end of trouble. This isn't just about you pissing on my feet. You're soaking everybody. So, what if I offer you a deal? Just between the two of us, aye? You back the fuck off and give us what you have on Daniel Robertson."

"What's in it for me?"

"You don't find yourself charged with obstructing police enquiries."

"You know I could walk that."

"Shit sticks. Think about your reputation. Your business."

I didn't even pretend to consider it. "This sounds like more than a pissing contest to me. You want to tell me why you're really so interested in Daniel Robertson?"

"Even I don't know, McNee. And do I give a flying fuck if you believe me or not? Think on this: would I come round just to hassle you? It's a waste of my time and yours."

"So you do this out of the kindness of your heart?"

Lindsay' lips curled: a grimace, not a smile. "Get to fuck."

"Say I agree; what do you suggest I tell my client?"

Lindsay raised his hands. "What do I care?" He walked past me. "I'll see myself out." He stopped in the doorway. "By the way, how's the leg?"

Chapter 6

Midnight.

My eyes were heavy, but my body refused to accept sleep. I'd tried turning in early. It hadn't worked.

Soon enough I'd realised what it was that was keeping me up, whispering around inside my head, preventing me from drifting off.

I was still dressed, lying on top of the covers.

I guess I already knew where I'd be going.

***

At the bridge, the guy in the booth took my money with a bored, limp gesture. Night shift. Every worker's bane.

There's an old joke that Fifers tell about the toll on the Road Bridge: people are happy paying to get out of Dundee but there's no way in hell they'd ever pay to go there.

I drove the back roads of Fife, my eyes focused on the roads ahead even though I could have made the journey blindfolded.

Some time later, I pulled the car over to the side of the road, two wheels up on the overgrown embankment. I climbed out, awkward, as always. Clambering like an idiot, my hands splayed on either side of the door for balance.

Tell me again that there's nothing wrong with my leg. Tell me again I came out of the accident un-fucking-scathed.

They'd rebuilt the dyke. The stones were new; perfectly smooth. I stood on the overgrown verge, ran my hands across the fresh stonework.

On the other side of the road, the trees stood close together; thick trunks casting dark shadows in the spaces between. Small animals rustled among dead grass and leaves, the light from the moon failing to penetrate those dark spaces.

Out here, there was no feeling of the city across the waters. No sense of encroaching industrialisation. No constant rush of traffic.

I closed my eyes. There were sounds more urgent than the call of animals and the gentle rustle of disturbed vegetation. But these other noises were merely echoes in my head from another time that I had not entirely left behind.

Dean Martin sang it: memories are made of this.

Memories.

I couldn't escape them.

Maybe I never really wanted to.

I opened my eyes again, blinked away the tears that had started to gather.

A voice in my head said: *She's gone.*

I had to keep reminding myself of that one simple fact. So easy to forget if I didn't keep thinking it: Elaine was dead.

Nothing could bring her back or atone for such a senseless fucking waste.

Something flitted in the shadows of the trees. Bats flew toward me from dark spaces. My muscles tensed, as if these tiny winged creatures might attack me. But they pulled away at the last instant, perfectly in control. They soared up above my head and circled in the sky, their forms silhouetted in the light of the moon, before returning to the trees.

I let out a long breath, watched it turn to mist.

I returned to the car, feeling sad but unburdened, as if something in that place had absorbed the pain that had been welling within me and preventing me from sleep.

My leg throbbed dully. When I pressed the accelerator, my calf muscles cramped.

***

Back home, I crashed on top of the bed again.

The flat was cold and empty. I had gone out to find her tonight, as though she would be waiting for me in that field. Telling me she was all right.

In the months after the accident I used to make that same journey, driving in a daze, half-asleep and functioning on auto-pilot. It was a wonder I never killed myself.

There were too many holes where memories used to be and I noticed every one of them. People told me I was maudlin to stay in the flat we had bought together, that I needed to move on.

I told them I would. When I was ready.

Chapter 7

Seven-fifteen a.m., I was dressed in dark jeans and a black t-shirt. Refreshed and ready for the day ahead.

My flat was to the west end of the city, in a refurbished tenement building. Close to a hundred years ago a one bedroom flat would have housed a whole family. Now even a two bedroom felt enclosed to a man who lived on his own.

The street itself was quiet enough. The neighbours, like me, kept themselves to themselves. Sometimes you saw kids from other buildings playing out on the streets. There's something reassuring about that.

Outside, I booted a stray football back to two young lads who were kicking about near the bottom of the street. They shot me a thumbs up. I kept walking.

I climbed in the car, threw on a CD. Larry Love drawled about being too sick to pray. I gunned the engine, pulled out and drove east to the city centre.

Ten minutes later, I parked across from my offices in a car park that may as well have been dirt land.

The land was due for renovation. Student accommodation. Once there had been division between the university and the town. Now it seemed as though one was taking over the other.

Progress. Even though I at least partially suspected the university admissions people had mistaken quantity for quality.

I locked the car, crossed the road. Bill was in at work already, sorting paperwork and making sure everything was shipshape.

He didn't look up when I came in. "You went home last night, then?"

I nodded.

"First time in a while." Refusing to look at me, seemingly intent on his work.

I didn't say anything, went straight through to my office.

Looking out the window as I waited for the computer to boot and the kettle to boil, I saw a dark blue Citroen C5 pull in next to my car. A woman got out the passenger's side, dressed in jeans and a thick jumper. Her dark hair was tied up and she wore thick, tortoise-shell glasses. I was too far away to make out intimate details but I knew the car. The woman, too.

Her husband climbed out. A small man, whose limbs twitched constantly as though he was wired up to the mains. He said something to her, and she shook her head, sadly. Then kissed him. Softly.

Some things never changed.

I thought about when I saw her in a hospital bed, her face pale and her eyes filled with mourning for a loss that I would never understand. How she had still seemed so much in control.

Like her sister. No mistaking that.

I walked away from the window, pressed my palms on the surface of the desk. Pushed all my weight down and took several deep breaths.

Why couldn't she just leave me alone? Let me deal with this in my own way?

Two minutes later, Bill knocked on the door. Hesitant.

"Let her in." As ready as I would ever be.

Rachel walked into my office. She was a small woman, slightly top-heavy, with sturdy legs. Dressed in thick clothes that swamped her frame. Her beauty was in her face; the skin perfectly smooth, the nose slim and petite, and the eyes a fragile shade of blue.

"We missed you," she said.

It was a lie. The "we" part, at least.

I didn't meet her gaze. "I've been busy. This whole business, you know, it's all new to me. Need a bit of time to get used to it, figure out a routine, you know?" I walked over and shook her hand. Stiff and polite. Awkward.

She took advantage, pulled me in for a hug and kissed me on the cheek.

I recoiled.

Regretted it.

She said, "The leg's looking better." When I didn't respond, she kept pressing. "Now you're just walking like your shoes don't fit properly."

I smiled. "They don't." I turned to the kettle. "Just boiled."

"If you're drinking."

I didn't say anything, just started making coffee.

She pushed past the barrier of small talk. "You should talk to him. I mean face to face." What the Americans would call a sucker-punch. Sneaked in when your guard is down. Guaranteed to knock you to the floor, keep you out for the count.

All the same, I retained my composure. At least, I tried. "I just don't think it's appropriate."

"Why?"

"Rach, the man thinks I killed his daughter."

Her face twitched as though she didn't know what kind of expression to settle on. "He was angry."

I almost said, "And maybe he's right," but kept that particular thought to myself.

"He told the police that I was the one responsible for the accident."

"He was looking for someone to—"

"Sure. We're all looking for someone to blame." Snapping it out there; enough force I could have knocked her out.

But Rachel was tough enough to take it. "If she was alive right now, she'd slap you silly."

No sneak attack. That was a direct hit. I turned away to make the coffee. Desperate not to meet her eyes. "I could never figure why she said yes to me." It sounded self-deprecatory even to my own ears.

"You came with her every year on her birthday. Five years, McNee. You were beginning to feel like family." She grinned, relaxing in nostalgia. "Except you wouldn't let us call you by your first name, huh, Ja—"

"Don't." I turned round, held up a warning finger. But found myself smiling all the same. Rachel did the same. I saw Elaine. The sly half grin and those sparkling eyes.

I passed her coffee. She took the cup in both hands, blew on the surface. Black liquid rippled. Waves crashed out to the lip of the mug. A storm in miniature.

"Elaine never called you by your first name? I find

that hard to believe. Even if you asked her to, I mean..."

"She understood me."

"She would have wanted you to talk to the old man."

There was sadness in Rachel's eyes, as though she thought there had been a terrible loss in this rupture between me and her father. "She wouldn't have wanted this to come between the two of you."

"Tell him that."

Rachel shook her head. "You're a cold bastard."

A sharp pain stabbed behind my forehead. "Is this why you came by? To have a pop at me? Thought your dad seemed to enjoy it so much, you'd have a try?"

"I wanted you to come with me. To see her."

"I can't."

"Why?"

Slamming the brakes on my anger, I found myself stuck with the same distance that I had greeted her with earlier.

"McNee, you're a fucking selfish prick, sometimes."

And she was gone, out the door and away.

I felt sick. Flopped into the chair she'd been using. Caught something faint in the air. A subtly sharp scent. My forehead was hot. That pain was getting worse; insistent. I wiped my head with the palm of my hand, felt the sweat slick away.

When I closed my eyes, ghosts danced indistinctly on the backs of my eyelids.

***

"You should be the one in the ground."

51

Martin Barrow's voice had been quiet, barely rising above the sound of the rain that battered on the mourners who had gathered that afternoon in the Balgay Cemetery to say their prayers for his daughter.

I had been standing at the rear of the assembled mourners. Hiding? And not just from him. But he'd been watching for me, I knew. He'd noticed the minute I slipped in.

People stepped away from us. Sensing his anger; maybe they even shared it.

I had thought about not attending. It would have been the easy option and who could have blamed me?

But I was there, and I had listened as the Reverend spoke softly about Elaine, and her mother held her husband's arm as though she might topple forward into the grave without the support.

"If you weren't the fuckin' police, they would have banged you up."

I tried not to respond.

"You killed her."

And I might have believed it was the response of a grieving parent had there not been this tiny voice in my head that whispered, *you know it's true.*

Chapter 8

I spent the afternoon buried in work. While there were other open cases, much of my time was consumed by Daniel Robertson.

The case fascinated me for many reasons. Not the least of which was the question of why Daniel had come home to kill himself. There was no emotional attachment left for him here. He had gone to great lengths to separate himself from his childhood and there was no reason why he would suddenly be overcome with a feeling of nostalgia.

I thought about the note he had written after his father's heart attack: "no worse than the old cunt deserves."

I asked myself: was his detachment an act?

There were other questions, too. Such as, why were the police treating an apparent suicide in such a hush-hush fashion?

But I typed up the report. There was no need for speculation in a professional investigation. James Robertson needed cold, hard facts. He was looking for closure. I wanted to deliver that.

It was early evening when the phone rang. Bill transferred it through from the front, telling me it was urgent.

"McNee." Rachel's voice was breathless. "It's Harry." Her husband. The ratty little man with the glasses who had been in the car with her that morning. "There was... Jesus, we were just having a drink and... he's been arrested." She didn't give me a chance to respond. "I know things didn't exactly go well this morning. But I could really do with someone here. And as selfish a fuck as I think you are at the moment, you're the only person I could think of."

* * *

It only took me two minutes to walk up the road. In the old days I would have entered through the main doors at the Marketgait, but I used the public entrance to the rear of the station. There was something intimidating about coming through that way. The shadow of FHQ fell accusingly and the entrance seemed hidden as though you wouldn't find it any other way than by deliberately looking for it.

I wondered if, when the building had been built back in the sixties, they had seen this aspect to it. Deliberately designed the building to intimidate.

Maybe they had at that; the remnants of old school Calvinism still running through the architect's genes, keeping their designs functional, joyless and overbearing.

If that was the case, why hadn't I seen it before?

Maybe it just felt different because, these days, I was no longer part of the system. Maybe it wasn't a Calvinist mindset so much as a copper's that had played a hand in the building's design.

Rachel was waiting outside, her arms folded across her stomach.

"Tell me," I said.

"I don't even... It was just meant to be a quiet couple of pints, you know?" Her face was pale, eyes turning bloodshot as she tried to hold back tears. "And then..."

"What happened?" Pressing her like I would a client, or a witness. Never mind what friendship we had, there was a reason she'd called me instead of someone else.

She looked at me with a hurt expression lurking behind her eyes. But it was gone in a moment. "We were just sitting there... and Harry... he went to get another couple of drinks. Knocked this guy at the bar."

"Bumped into him?"

"Yes."

"And he attacked Harry?"

"He said a few things. Harry told him to fuck off."

"Glaswegian manners." He'd been living in the city five years, but he always played his west coast hard man heritage to the hilt.

She managed to smile. "Says the man from Dundee, yeah?"

She looked away from me and ran a hand through her hair before wrapping her arms round her middle once more. She shifted her weight from foot to foot.

"Harry calls you Dundee McNee, you know that?"

"The name's a curse."

"Maybe."

"At least the family name's not Hunt."

She nodded. Hadn't heard me.

I realised, then, that she'd asked me here not for

55

comfort but for distraction. To have someone to talk to. Not about this, of course. About anything but this.

All the same, I didn't back down.

"Tell me what happened."

"That should have been it, right? Harry telling him to fuck off. But he makes a deal out of it, you know? Keeps telling Harry he could have him in a fight."

"So Harry lamps him?"

"No. Not then."

"But that's why we're here."

"Do you want to know what happened or are you just going to make up your own mind?"

Recently, I didn't seem to be able to help jumping to conclusions about people. I'd done it with James Robertson when I saw his flushed face and his large frame, and again to Kat when I saw her mutton-dressed-as-lamb fashion sense.

And now I was judging Harry on the man I knew he had been rather than on the man he had become. The man Rachel loved.

"Harry came back to the table. Just sat down, tried to enjoy his pint. But the man wouldn't let up. Came over, taunting Harry. Then turned to me, said... some inappropriate things."

"So Harry really did hit him."

"You can't say it was unprovoked."

"Maybe."

"Definitely."

"It could happen anywhere..."

The doors opened. Someone came outside, lit from behind so that their features were obscured. "Excuse me, Rach..."

I tried to smile in greeting. Found it hard to even approximate.

Police Constable Susan Bright took a step backwards. Not a conscious move, but that didn't make any difference. We hadn't spoken in eight or nine months.

"Susan," I said, making an attempt to be friendly.

"McNee... What are you...?"

"She's Elaine's sister." They'd known each other in passing, Elaine and Susan.

Susan looked good. Not that I'd expected a matter of months to age her, but all the same she seemed in good shape and her new hairstyle — bobbed short, almost severe — gave her an air of confidence.

"I'm sorry, Steed, I didn't think that..." For a second I saw something of the woman I used to know in her. The use of my old nickname was what did it, I suppose. Gave her words a kind of fondness I'd almost forgotten.

"So Harry's in trouble?" I said.

"You know who he punched out? Frank Beaney."

"Aye? That chancer?"

She laughed. "Guess Frank thought he was a hard man today."

"How many pints convinced him of that?"

Susan's stance changed suddenly, as though she'd remembered she was here in a professional capacity. She turned to Rachel, looking past me as though I no longer existed. "I'm sorry... We shouldn't be laughing. I came out here to tell you we'll be letting your husband go. With a caution, of course."

"Of course."

"All things considered... Harry seems quite happy to forget the incident."

"I am, as well."

"He should be out in a few minutes."

Rachel nodded. "Thank you."

As Susan slipped back inside again, she nodded curtly in my direction. "Steed," she said. I remembered when the name had been friendly, like a kind of private joke between us. This time, it sounded more like a habit. The only name she could think to call me.

Rachel looked at me strangely. "You were friends. Better friends than—"

"Emphasis on the 'were'."

"You want to tell me what 'Steed' is all about?"

I shrugged, made light of it. "As in Patrick MacNee. *The Avengers*."

"That's it?"

"That's it."

She studied me for a few seconds. "You don't strike me as an umbrella man. And you're definitely not one for nicknames."

"Guess that's why it kind of faded away."

"For some people," she said.

I couldn't meet her gaze. I felt oddly embarrassed, as though she'd read something into the nickname she shouldn't have.

"I'm sorry I called you out."

"You shouldn't be."

She shook her head. "But I am. This was nothing and I know..."

"I mean it," I said.

"We always used to ask her how she could stand you," Rachel said. A smile tugged at her lips, faintly nostalgic. "I mean, how she could take the hot and cold running emotion..." She caught my gaze, held it as though trying to see if I understood what she was talking about. "One minute, you're there in the bosom of the family and the next you won't even talk to any of us. Even those of us who know that it wasn't your fault."

I couldn't do anything but shrug in response to that. Guilty as charged. And nothing I could do about it, either.

The door opened. Harry stumbled out, hugged his wife. "You all right?"

She murmured something and held him tight.

I stood back.

When they stepped apart, Harry extended his hand. "McNee," he said. "It's been a while."

"Aye."

"Since the funeral."

I thought about punching his lights out. Instead, I nodded. "I hear you restrained yourself tonight."

He tried looking genial. "All of that's behind me."

"Aye?"

"We should get home," Rachel said. "It's been a long night."

Harry looked at me as though expecting a parting shot. I gave him nothing.

Rachel kissed me on the cheek. "Thank you," she said.

By the time I even thought about replying, they were out of earshot.

Chapter 9

My mobile rang the next morning, dragging me from sleep. I reached out and grabbed the phone off the table.

"It looks like I no longer require your services, Mr McNee," Robertson said.

I answered blearily, "I was going to call you later today, hand over my report on—"

"My brother, the London gangster? I know, Mr McNee. Kat — his girlfriend — she told me all about it."

"Mr Robertson, I was holding off until I could confirm certain information. You wanted to know why your brother committed suicide?"

"I know everything I need to know, McNee. The bastard topped himself because he finally took responsibility for who he was. How much more does a man need to know than what she had to tell me? What, you were wanting to see if you could find anything else? Because you weren't already sure he'd become a bloody monster, aye? Like there was some deeper reason for him to go hang himself? You're a bloody parasite. Spinning this thing out so you could keep taking my money."

I wasn't so sure about the reasons Daniel Robertson had killed himself, but I kept quiet. I didn't know how to tell his brother that I didn't think Daniel felt any remorse for the people he'd hurt, the terrible things he'd done.

"You deliver your report, McNee," he said. "And I'll pay yer bloody bills."

Five minutes later, in the shower, my thoughts began to organise themselves.

DI Lindsay and his little visit to my office, warning me off the case.

Everything raising my suspicions.

The shower battered the paranoia out of my brain.

And then, out of nowhere, I found myself thinking about Constable Susan Bright. How she looked when I saw her in the hospital. Distance in her eyes. Maybe even a kind of hatred.

Not that I could blame her.

Memories...

Of skin slick with sweat and a sick guilt that crept up on me in the night.

In the hospital, Rachel had called her cold. But there had been a time when Susan would greet me with fond affection.

Before I fucked her over.

Out of the shower, I towelled down. Dressed for the day.

My leg was stiff. My crutches sat in a cupboard, waiting.

I pulled them out, thinking; maybe just for a day or two. Take the load off.

But I had to walk on my own. Who needed a crutch?

The phone rang again.

"Get your arse over here, now," Lindsay said.

"I think you've got the wrong number."

"Park Place, you cocky shite. Now. There's a woman here, and let me tell you, pal, she's got your fuckin' number."

***

The entrance was sealed off with crime scene tape. Beat officers scurried about like someone was going to kick their arses if they dared stand still.

The building itself was nothing to write home about. No security entrance. Old fashioned sash windows, one of the upper floors using cellophane instead of glass. The kind of place the tourist board keeps out of the brochures.

A constable clamped a beefy hand on my shoulder. His weight made me buckle, almost sent me down. I'd left the crutches at home. "You can't go in there."

"I'm here to see DI Lindsay." Keep standing. Make it look natural.

"Name?" He reminded me of Lurch from the Addams family. Same monosyllabic sentence structure. Same stature. His hair was combed forward in a mock-Beatles cut. His large nose jutted out from his face like a badly chipped lump of granite.

I gave him my full name. He nodded slowly. "Aye, he said you'd be here."

We walked up to the second floor.

The door of the flat had been knocked off its hinges. Green paint peeled, revealing the dirty white undercoat. There had been a number painted on the letterbox once, but it had faded to a ghostly imprint. The wooden surround was splintered and cracked.

Lindsay was smoking a cigarette. The scent was strong, but couldn't mask the dank musk of the close's natural odour. The bags under his eyes told me he hadn't got much sleep the night before. So did the rumpled suit, the same one he'd been wearing yesterday.

"Glad you could make it."

Aye, I thought. That'll be right.

"What do you want?"

He dropped the cigarette and stubbed it out with his heel. "Come in." Lifted the yellow tape.

I followed him down the corridor. The wallpaper was off-white. Faint pale-yellow stripes ran from ceiling to floor. No photos on the wall. No personal touches. No carpets, even.

A smell lingered in the air: rotten, acidic.

He took me into what must have been the living room. The same wallpaper. A raggedy sofa was pushed back against the far wall. A small, black and white TV balanced on a wooden box under the window. The rug that was chucked down in the middle of the room was thick and dirty with decorative Chinese symbols woven into the fabric.

And dumped on that: the body.

Face down. Arms and legs uncomfortably twisted. Abandoned with little thought for aesthetics.

A man in protective plastics snapped away at the scene with his camera.

"Anyone you know?" Lindsay asked.

The woman who had called herself Kat had been left half-naked. Her upper body was a mess of ugly bruising and vicious, open wounds.

I walked round the rug, treating the edges like a barrier I couldn't cross.

The back of her head was a mess of blood and bone.

It was hard to equate with anything that had once been a human skull.

It was only when I saw her face that my stomach tried to escape through my throat.

There was a ragged hole in her head, just above the bridge of her nose. The edges were blackened with dried blood and powder residue. Below that, her eyes were open.

"We found your card," said Lindsay. "On the carpet next to her. Someone wanted us to see it. What was she to you? A client?"

"No."

"Then what?"

"She could have picked up my card anywhere." Lying instinctively. Lindsay had a way of bringing out the worst in me.

"So you're saying you didn't know this woman?"

I stepped forward but Lindsay placed a hand on my chest, stopped me from approaching her. "You can't interfere with a crime scene while the geeks are examining the area." The guy with the camera glanced up, irritation and insult plain on his face.

"I did know her," I admitted. "At least I've met her once before."

Lindsay didn't seem fazed that I'd lied to him earlier. "Care to share?"

In the office, she'd seemed nervous. Perhaps her death had not been entirely unexpected.

I told him what I could.

"This old tart was Daniel Robertson's... girlfriend?"

"Yeah," I said. "This... old tart." I could have lamped him. She deserved some respect in death. But I knew I had to pick my battles, and nothing would be accomplished by pulling Lindsay up on respect. Empathy wasn't high on his list of personality traits.

Of course, personality wasn't exactly up there, either.

"So why come to you?"

A good question.

"She must have traced Daniel here, somehow. Maybe she thought he'd be coming back home."

Lindsay regarded me with a strange expression. "So she came up here because she thought lover boy had jilted her? She wanted to confront him? Give him a smack in the pus, maybe, tell him he was an arsehole, and then go home?"

"Something like that, I guess."

"Or she wanted to find him, try and talk some sense into the bawbag. Persuade him to come home. Aye, I suppose that could be it. Daniel Robertson was a real catch."

"Love is funny like that," I said. "Makes you do strange things."

Lindsay didn't reply. He kept looking at the body on the floor, blinking with every camera flash.

I thought about James Robertson calling me earlier. Remembered his voice. The way he talked about her. That vicious tone.

What did he think when he saw her? Dolled up in her fake furs, hiding her natural features beneath thick make-up. A mask, perhaps, but my client wouldn't see it that way.

The James Robertson I knew was a conservative thinker. Judged on appearance, used his own self-image as a moral yardstick. This woman would never have met his expectations. But then, Daniel Robertson's life seemed to be entirely at odds with his brother's ideals.

The photographer finished his work and stepped back, letting two other men in surgical gear approach. They unrolled a stretcher, lifted her body.

She looked unreal. Oddly artificial.

When they took her out of the room, acid churned in my stomach. My mind flashed on a similar scene. Feelings that had left me hollowed out and empty.

Lindsay said, "So you were the one introduced her to the brother?"

I nodded. Told him about their meeting the night before.

"You were with them when they met?"

"No. I offered my services, but this was something he had to do on his own."

"Did he say where they were going to meet?"

"Mennies. On the Perth Road."

Lindsay knew the pub, nodded. Seemed to wait on me saying something more.

I locked eyes with him. "Something else you want?"

Lindsay shook his head. "You're free to go." I made to walk past him, but he grabbed me roughly by the elbow. "Stay available. We're done talking for now. But I have a feeling we'll talk again soon enough."

I shook off his grip. "It's a date," I said and resisted the urge to give him the finger on my way out the door.

On the street, I walked round the corner and leaned against the brick wall of a building for support. My leg had caught fire and I felt close to tears.

Chapter 10

I was leaning against the stone dyke that ran along the banks of the Tay. I looked left, down the length of the road bridge that spanned the water. On the far banks of the river, small towns nestled peacefully in the Fife countryside. Newport, Tayport, others.

The air that came in off the river carried a gentle tang; an unobtrusive scent skimming from the surface of the water. I breathed it in.

Gulls flew above the water, cackling like lunatics.

I turned my gaze to the rail bridge which stood further west, down the meandering path of the river.

The original bridge had collapsed in 1879, barely a year after construction had finished. A storm shook the bridge's foundation and a passenger train had plunged into the darkness of the water below.

The train itself was later dredged from the river and, amazingly, returned to active service. Its passengers were not so lucky. Sometimes, when I walked by the river at night and the moon was just right, I saw the victims of the disaster shifting below the surface of the water, reaching up towards the surface, their fingers clawed and their faces stretched in terror.

Today was a beautiful day, however, and the waters were calm. Any ghosts lurking below the surface were quiet. Maybe they were even content down there in the peaceful deep. It would have been easy to join them. Simply close my eyes and go to sleep as the water gently flowed around me.

I pushed such thoughts away, pulled out my mobile and dialled through to the daytime number Robertson had given me.

"Aye?" he said.

"It's me."

"I'm not paying a penny till I see that report, McNee."

"Have the police contacted you?"

"No. Why?"

I took a deep breath. "We need to talk. Are you at home?"

"I'm in town."

"Where are you now?" I asked. When he told me, I said, "I'll meet you at the café in Tesco by the Riverside. Five minutes."

When I hung up, my mind flashed on Kat's corpse. Closed in on details I could never have seen.

Fist against flesh.

A knife slicked with blood.

Her eyes wide with fear.

The muzzle of a gun pressed hard against her forehead, whitening the surrounding skin.

My muscles tightened. My breathing became harsh.

It was a familiar sensation, one I thought I had left behind long ago. The world drifted away. My muscles contracted. Leaving me with fingers and toes curled into tight fists that refused to open again.

Pins and needles ran up and down my legs. Although I was leaning on the stone wall for support, it felt flimsy. Ready to collapse, send me hurtling over and into the water.

I concentrated on the ice in my lungs. Forced myself to take each breath slowly and carefully. Ignoring the signals that my brain was sending, forcing me to take in shallow gulps of oxygen.

I focused on the cold stone beneath my hands. Made that sensation my anchor to reality. One thing to keep me conscious of where I was and what was happening.

Slowly, my senses came back. The bubbles in my head popped. My breathing, still ragged, slowed and the ice in my lungs melted. The pain left me. My hands and feet tingled as though alive with electricity.

How long since I had felt like this?

Hard to recall. Since I was teenager? Later?

I remembered the doctor calling it "growing pains" and when I reached my twenties, it was easy to believe he'd been right. So why, if that was true, had it come back now?

As if I needed to look hard for the answer to that.

I moved the weight off my left leg.

I bit my lower lip. The wind grew cold.

My imagination?

Chapter 11

Robertson bit into the bacon roll. Flour exploded. Tomato sauce oozed. Teeth clamped hard. I thought of a knife-edge tearing through Kat's skin. Around us, families relaxed in the middle of their weekly shop. High windows on three sides of the café let natural light into the building. The coffee machine kept up a constant background noise.

I sipped at my coffee: boiled water. No bite.

Robertson chewed and swallowed. "So tell me," he said. As his lips moved I saw flecks of sauce and meat on his teeth. "Why do the police want to talk to me?"

"Tell me what happened the other night."

His eyes narrowed. "Told you everything you needed to know over the phone."

"She told you about the man your brother became," I said. "A criminal. A brawler, a drug dealer, maybe worse."

"I'm not a violent man. But keep talking that way about Daniel and maybe that'll be put to the test."

Two tables away, a baby started to cry. Its mother,

a young woman with peroxide-blonde hair and giant, gold-hooped earrings, tried to quiet it by forcing a bottle against the child's lips. Its screams pierced my ears. I wanted to get up, shake the little bastard, get him to shut his face.

I concentrated on what my client had to tell me. Professionalism.

I leaned across the table.

"Tell me what happened."

Robertson put down his roll. "What's this about?"

"Tell me."

He looked ready to protest again, but his expression softened.

And he told me.

***

He didn't give much away.

I wasn't there, of course. All I had to go on was his version of events. And even if he told me something of how he felt, he stuck rigidly to the facts. No meandering. No asides.

Had he rehearsed this tale?

The Speedwell Bar on the Perth Road is more popularly known to the locals as Mennies after the family who owned the pub from the early 20s through to 1995 when it was finally sold on to a private owner. Robertson had chosen it as a meeting place. Because he didn't want to be alone with this woman. And because he knew he'd need a stiff drink.

Real beer. Proper whisky.

The kind of drinks Mennies had built its reputation on.

Robertson had a photograph of himself and his brother as teenagers, before all the trouble had broken out with their father; back when they had been inseparable. He hadn't looked at it in decades. It had been kept in a box, packed away like other remembrances.

He had brought it with him to the pub. Laid it on the table in one of the quieter side rooms while he supped at his pint and waited for Kat to arrive.

So she'd recognise him?

Or for his own comfort?

The bar was hoaching, he said. The crowd made him feel more at ease.

Maybe I understood something of that, how it was easier to disappear into a crowd. You could let them distract you from yourself so easily.

Finally a woman's hand placed itself across the photograph. The index finger touched against his brother's right cheek; a caress.

Robertson looked up and saw Kat standing at the table.

"You look like him," she said, sitting across from him. "I mean, you're bigger, and I think maybe life's been a little kinder to you, but still, you can see it."

"You were his girlfriend?"

She giggled and then placed her hand over her mouth. "I'm sorry. It's all a little much sometimes, yeah?" She composed herself. "I was his girlfriend, his lover, however you want to say it."

"He never mentioned you in his letters." He shrugged. "Well, never mentioned much in his letters." Then, standing up: "You want a drink?"

"Yeah," she said. "That'd be nice. Vodka and Coke, love, if you'd be so kind."

When he got back to the table Kat was holding the photo, studying it with a dedicated intensity.

He set down her drink in front of her. She reacted

like his arrival had shocked her out of sleep.

"I was just thinking about him. How much he meant to me." She forced a smile. "That photo, you were both very handsome boys."

"How long were you and my brother...?"

"Two years. On and off. Our lives didn't make things easy."

Looking at her, Robertson tried to see some sign that she hadn't loved Daniel. And the more he looked in her eyes, the more he saw a deep sadness. He paused in his story and stared at me. The more he looked in her eyes, he said, the more he found he hated her.

I nodded. I sort of understood.

He continued: "He never told me much about what he did," he'd said to Kat.

"Yeah?" she said. "Not surprising, I guess. You do what you can to get by."

Robertson was worried by this; a sick feeling in his gut like she was about to finally destroy any hope he had for his brother.

"And what did he do?"

Kat put the photo face down on the wooden table, took a deep breath and then told him about the life of Daniel Robertson.

***

Robertson looked like he couldn't go on. Just remembering what she had said was enough to upset him.

"What did she tell you?"

He started to say something, but stumbled.

"What did she tell you?"

"She told me about how he worked for this man in London. How he broke people's arms when they didn't pay debts. How he killed men because they interfered with his boss's business. She told me about his jail time."

"I'm sorry..." The words my mantra of the past few days. Everyone's life going to shite, and all I could do was repeat two meaningless little sounds.

"Aye, like hell, you parasitic bastard. How much money were you going to bleed before you finally told me the truth?"

"These things take time. I needed to verify—"

"Save it. Bloody leech!"

"That was all you talked about? Your brother, his life?"

"Aye. Now would you tell me..."

There was no way to break it gently: "Last night, someone killed her. Her body was discovered in a dingy wee flat in the east end. She'd been assaulted and murdered."

Blood drained — as best it could — from his face.

"She was stabbed. And finally, a bullet through the head. The police know about your meeting."

"You told them?"

"At the scene, they found one of my business cards. It had been left there. Deliberately, I'd say."

"...who...?"

"I don't know."

"Did you tell the bloody police I killed her?"

I shook my head. "If you say you're innocent, then I believe you. But you have to be prepared. You were in the right place at the right time. You have a credible motive in the eyes of the police. You —"

"I'm not a killer." Spitting the words.

"They'll want to talk to you," I said. "To know everything that happened. It's not going to be easy on you. They make sure it never is."

"I'd have no reason to…"

"I need you to be honest with me. When she told you about Daniel… did you…?"

"Lose the plot? Aye, bloody right I did."

"What happened?"

"Nothing."

He pushed the half finished bacon roll across the table.

I waited.

"We had a wee barney at the table," he said. "I called her a few names."

"Witnesses?"

"It was bloody Mennies, of course there were witnesses."

"Did you leave together?"

"I left before her."

"You left the bar first?"

"That's what I just said." He hung his head forward and rubbed his palms hard against his face.

I sat back and looked at him. Trying to gain a full picture of the man. Trying to understand him.

Old instincts and training took over.

Interview techniques:

Consider the facts.

Line them up with your gut feeling.

Catch your suspect out in a lie.

If you can't do that, then re-asses your position.

Analyse everything.

Detach yourself.

Whoever killed Kat had done so with deliberate care and attention. This was not the work of an amateur.

Mennies was to the west of the city. The flat where her body had been discovered was to the east. If her death was a crime of passion — and if Robertson was

the killer, I could think of no other explanation —
then the body dump made no sense. The distance
between the two locations was such that she had
either gone willingly or been taken by force.

And then there was the question of why that flat?
Why that location? Robertson had no connection to
the building.

So who did?

Knowing how easy it had been for Kat to trace
Daniel to Dundee, I began to wonder if perhaps
someone had followed her.

I was watching Robertson, not allowing myself to
empathise. Just observing.

"I need to know if you noticed anyone else last
night."

"What do you mean?"

"In the pub. Anyone who stood out. Who showed
an unnatural interest in you or Kat. I mean if they
were just watching or if they tried to talk to you… or
if you saw anyone talking to her after you—"

"There was no one! Jesus Christ, there was no one,
all right?"

He tried not to cry in front of me. But his skin red-
dened and his body shook.

And a flash of familiarity burned across my brain
as I watched, but I pushed that away until there was
nothing left but the cool, uninvolved observer, who
did nothing but watch, analyse and consider.

Chapter 12

We walked along Riverside. A cool breeze blew in from the west.

Robertson said, "Do I just hand myself over, then?"

I shook my head. "Wait for them to come to you. You're the last person to be seen with her. That makes you a suspect. It doesn't make you guilty. You shouldn't be acting like it does, either."

He laughed at that. "Come on, you can't be that naïve." His face creased. Close to tears. "I'm not a bad man. All I ever wanted was to keep my father's farm running." He dug his hands deep into the pockets of his padded green jacket. "My son doesn't want anything to do with it, of course. Different generation, aye? He lives with his mother and her fancy man in Glasgow. He was a real farm lad when he was young, but since she took him out there he grew soft. Wants to be a musician, now. His band, they're no actually all that bad. For what they are. But music's no life for anyone. And that noise they play, it's all drugs and pissing away your good health."

I didn't say anything, thought of my own wasted youth.

We passed a small parking spot where two fishermen had set up their equipment against the dyke. They cast their lines into the Tay, watching the waters closely, neither man saying a word to the other.

Robertson looked at the men as we walked past and a faint smile played across his features. "Me and Daniel, when we were bairns, we used to go fishing at this wee pond near the house. A puddle, really, but to us it was amazing. Fish used to come in off this stream. Piddling wee things, but it didn't matter." His eyes took on the glaze of nostalgia.

There was a ringing from Robertson's pocket. He scowled, answered. The conversation was brief and one sided. Robertson listened, mostly. When he hung up, he turned to me and said, "You were right. That was one of the lads who works on the farm. The police have been round asking after me." He took a deep breath. "That woman was a tramp. A bloody whore. No question about it. I don't want to speak ill of the dead, but you could see it all over her. She didn't love my brother. No matter how much she tried to tell me otherwise. All the same, she didn't deserve to die."

I noticed for the first time how tired he looked.

Robertson turned away from me, looked out at the Rail Bridge. A train was passing over, away from the city. Robertson watched it leave.

"Nobody," he said, "deserves to die."

***

I offered to accompany Robertson back home, but he refused. Saying he'd deal with this on his own. Still angry with me. He wrote out a cheque to cover the work I'd already completed.

I watched him closely as he signed his name, this fat farmer with his bunnet and his scowl.

I'd treated him as cordially as possible. Maybe even felt sympathy. But none of that detracted from the fact he was a prick.

His brother's life as a gangster only worried him because of the way it made him look. In his mind, the worst case scenario was: what kind of shame can Daniel bring to my name and to my family?

And his reaction to Kat: shame. This was not a woman Robertson could ever have approved of. His brother's whore.

Even his attitude towards his son was old fashioned and disappointed; one sentence away from calling the boy a hippie, saying he should get his hair cut.

I should have been happy to get rid of him.

Except there were still unanswered questions.

One of the most important was why Daniel killed himself.

There was no adequate explanation. If I believed Kat, he just didn't have it in him.

Besides, a suicide didn't fit the image of the unrepentant hard man, and it seemed strange that his actions had taken his lover so completely by surprise.

His lover, who was now dead.

Murdered. No question, there.

After I left Robertson, I took the long route back to the office. Hoping the walk might clear my mind.

I tried thinking about other cases. Insurance jobs. Internet traces.

The Robertson case was at a dead end. It was a police matter, now.

Except I couldn't stop thinking about it.

Rachel had called. Asked me to meet her at Mickey Coyle's on the Old Hawkhill, round the back of the university campus. An old brick building that was in danger of being swallowed up as the university expanded.

We sat in a nook near the window, ordered lunch and drinks. She drank soda water and lime.

Elaine's drink.

We sipped slowly. Over the stereo, Rod Stewart and the Faces played at a low volume.

I tried to think of something to say. An opening gambit that would dispel the awkwardness we both felt.

She sat on the inside, underneath the window. If I looked past her I could see the outside world between the slats of the blinds. The skies were grey and the city illuminated by a dull light.

Finally, I asked: "How is he?"

She took a moment to respond. "Harry? He's good. All things considered." There was some accusation in her voice. But I couldn't pick up the specifics.

Some fucking investigator I was.

"He's a changed man, you know."

I didn't know what to say. I nodded, as though I believed her.

"He grew up in a tough place. And he got out. He became someone else. He paid the price for what he did when he was young. And he got over it. Even if some people never believed that."

When Rachel had lost her baby, I'd believed that Harry was responsible. I'd known about his chequered past. He'd spent a few years in prison for assault. And I held it against him.

I remembered seeing him in the hospital, looking at her with such love and adoration and feeling myself burn inside when I realised what I'd thought him capable of.

Because I knew when I saw that look on his face that I'd been wrong. I saw the way she looked at him and realised that she had been telling the truth. It was no one's fault she had lost her child.

And maybe that made it worse on her.

I thought of myself as cool, calm and detached. Put up a good front, too. And then I did something like that, judging a man in a moment. Letting anger dictate my actions.

Outside the station, I'd almost done it again. Assuming he was guilty.

Rachel never assumed. She loved her husband, seeing past who he had been to the man he really was.

Rachel and her sister: so close, so alike. Elaine had done the same for me. Seen something no one else could.

"Aye, everything sorts out," I said after a pause that went on too long. And instantly hated myself for doling out platitudes to someone I cared for.

Rachel looked at me strangely, as though I'd just given away something she'd never expected.

But I was saved by the barman bringing over our meals.

I dug into the steak pie. Rachel ate her chilli with deliberation while the air between us settled.

"I guess you sorted things out, you and Harry."

She shook her head. "We moved on. That's what you do. You deal with things and move on. And what happened, in the end it was nobody's fault."

"He's alright. For a Weegie prick."

She smiled at that. The smile turned into a laugh. Her eyes sparkled and her lips parted, displaying perfectly formed teeth. Then she stopped and frowned as if puzzling over a particularly tricky problem. She looked at me with her head cocked to one side. That same look she'd given me just a few minutes earlier. "I never really got it. What she saw in you."

"Neither did I. I was just grateful."

"But right there," she said. "Just for a moment, maybe I saw something." She looked at the surface of the table, her expression that of an embarrassed schoolgirl. "Sometimes, McNee, I might believe you're as human as the rest of us."

Chapter 13

Driving past St Michaels you would hardly notice it, except for the pub that sits on the junction right at the heart of the hamlet. The St Michaels Inn has a local reputation, well deserved, for good food and a relaxed atmosphere.

Other than that, there isn't much to the place. A few houses nearby. The forest just across the way. A smattering of houses with a main road running between them.

I parked the car outside the inn as the weather began to clear. The sun wasn't looking to show its head, but the temperature was pleasant.

Walking into the lounge, I noticed a middle-aged man in a checked shirt and blue jeans playing darts on his own. Tucked into a corner table, a young couple dressed in walking gear shared a quiet pint.

The barman was in his early twenties, maybe even late teens, with fair hair gelled into the approximation of a hedgehog. His face was open, honest and welcoming. The kind of face a family pub like St

Michaels probably relied on. He was soft spoken, polite and deferential when he said hello. I ordered a Stella. As he pulled my pint, I said, "You know James Robertson?"

"Thought that story was dead."

"Sorry?"

"You're a reporter, right?"

I shook my head, pulled a business card from my wallet. He examined it closely, pursing his lips and nodding.

"So what has this got to do with Mister Robertson?" he asked, handing me my pint and slipping the card into the breast pocket of his shirt. His eyes lit up. For this lad, there was whiff of danger and excitement about a job he'd only seen people do on the telly.

"I'm working for a private client. Clearing up a few loose ends." Conspiratorial.

"Aye? Like what?" The lad bought it without question.

"Like why Robertson's brother committed suicide."

He nodded. "It's a puzzler. I didn't know he had family. Except his son and ex, like. All I know is he likes to come in for a pint every now and then. I think he takes a wee walk across his fields, just to check everything's okay, you know, and pops in for a quick pick-me-up."

"But you know him well enough?"

"Local man," he said. "In a place like this you get to know everyone in a ten-mile radius."

"But not too well?"

"We're not buddies, no," said the lad. "I don't really know much of his business, like. Just the usual pub talk." He leaned over the bar. "What is this about, huh?"

"I want to get to know him, you know? Understand him a little better."

"You could try talking to him." As if it was the most obvious thing in the world.

I tapped the side of my nose. "I need to know him without, uh, knowing him." The lad didn't even realise I was playing him. Would he have answered these questions from anyone else?

"He's not an unfriendly man," he said. "A bit stand offish, I guess. You know, I'm behind the bar, he's getting a drink and that's it. Even if he is in here every night. His wife left him about six years ago."

"Before your time," I said, not even bothering to make it a question.

"Aye, well," said the lad. "I've only worked here about a year, now."

"But you know about the divorce."

"Sure. The old hands, they let you know about regulars when you start. They said his wife was one hell of a battleaxe."

"So everyone expected him to start chasing after the local talent?"

That earned me a grin. "Aye, well, you haven't seen some of the lasses that work here at nights, huh?"

I raised my eyebrows; I knew what he was talking about.

"Some people, even the happily married ones, like, they get a little frisky sometimes. Harmless banter, mostly. All the same Mr Robertson, he's not like that."

"He's not interested?"

"I guess. Not like he's, you know, gay or anything, like. Just that it doesn't matter to him."

"He was never frisky. How about aggressive?"

"Not really in his nature," said the lad. "I've never seen him get excited one way or the other. Most nights, he'll come in, grab a pint and sit in a corner. If someone talks to him, he'll talk back a bit, but mostly I think he just wants to be on his own. Enjoy his pint, you know?" His curiosity about my business with Robertson and the death of his brother still wasn't sated. "Seriously, man, you can tell me what this is all about. I'm the soul of discretion."

I drained the pint, paid him and made to leave.

"You need anything else, come back," said the lad as I was halfway out the door. "Ask for Ally."

***

It was coming on for half four. The weather had degenerated once more to dull grey and the warmth from earlier had been replaced by a nip that made me dig my hands into my pockets and pull my jacket tight around me. There was the hint of rain in the air. My skin goosepimpled. Thunder threatened for later in the evening.

My leg muscles felt stiff as I walked out of the car park, crossed the road and followed the edge of the forest. Bird calls echoed in the open air. Occasionally the rumble of traffic tumbled from the main road, which was hidden by a thick line of trees.

I thought about Kat.

I should have known. Should have protected her. I heard her on the phone, how she reacted to those other voices. I knew the kind of man Robertson had been, the kind of men she must have known.

I'd failed her while she was alive. I couldn't afford to do it again now that she was dead.

When I had taken the ABI courses after leaving the force, I kept insisting that I was simply moving into another area of law enforcement. A good percentage of investigators, after all, are ex-coppers.

The course leader had been quick to stress that there were differences between policing and private investigation.

"Investigators don't solve crimes. We don't arrest people. We don't get involved with murder. We can uncover the truth. We can help prevent crime. Provide security, perhaps. Assist police with their inquiries. Gain evidence on behalf of solicitors or private clients. But our powers don't extend to police work. Wherever possible we work with law enforcement agencies rather than against them."

That last statement was lip service. After all, they didn't want to work with us, so why should we work with them?

When Robertson cut me loose, my professional interest in him, his brother and Kat's murder should have ended.

I should have banked the cheque. There were other cases, other clients.

But I realised that I felt a sense of responsibility for what I saw as the fallout from my investigation.

If I had not made that one phone call, Kat would never have come to Dundee. She might still be alive.

All I wanted was to rectify my own mistake. Anything I found, I told myself, I'd take to Lindsay. To hell with my personal feelings, I wasn't equipped to handle something like this.

Funny thing was, I hadn't even liked Kat.

And yet, here I was.

There was a connection between her death and Daniel's suicide. I could feel it. Tantalisingly close but just beyond my reach. I had to go back. Examine everything.

And it all started with a body swinging from a tree.

***

I took the path Robertson had walked on the evening he discovered his brother's corpse. Followed it slowly.

Walked past the remains of crime scene tape left scattered by the side of the path. Caught up in the undergrowth. An ugly reminder of what had happened here.

I stepped off the path, pushed past thick branches and leaves.

In front of me stood the tree where Daniel Robertson's corpse had been found. A black, ugly mockery of nature that erupted from the earth as though it had clawed its way up from hell, the tree stood there, a dead thing in the centre of the living forest. Leaves carpeted the muddy ground at its base. They cracked and broke beneath my weight.

I closed my eyes, tried to visualise the body that had swung from the blackened branches.

The wind picked up.

The silhouette of Daniel's corpse appeared and disappeared like a ghost who didn't want to be seen. Even my mental image of the tree slowly melted away to be replaced by some other scene of horror.

Painted on the back of my eyelids: Kat on the rug. When they turned her over I saw a face that I thought was becoming familiar again these past few days.

It wasn't real, I knew, but no matter how hard I tried, I kept seeing Elaine's face imposed on that battered, broken body. And her expression was alive with a sadness that took my breath away.

Chapter 14

"You want to tell me what this is about?"

I didn't quite know how to answer. "I hear you're on Lindsay's team."

"I'm looking to join CID. Get a promotion to DS."

"You'd be good."

"Thank you."

"I mean it."

I had called Susan that afternoon. We had met at the University Quadrangle. Most of the students were home for the summer. The place was sheltered. Peaceful.

On four sides, Victorian buildings enclosed us. Plant life grew thick and beautiful, soaking up the sun.

Her long fringe fell forward and covered her face.

"This isn't about catching up. It's about the dead woman?"

I thought I might as well be honest. "Aye."

"Lindsay went off on one earlier. Told me that he didn't give a shite if we were still friends. If you

89

started sniffing around, I was to give you a smack in the pus and tell you to go home. That's a fairly direct quote."

"Well?"

She shook her head. "It's none of your concern. The suicide. The murder. Any of it."

"I know that."

"So why?"

"My client feels terrible about what happened."

"We went to see him this afternoon. Just for a chat. All the same, he seemed prepared. Like someone had coached him. That was you?"

"Uh-huh."

"Lindsay's going to want your head on a platter."

"Sure. Like he didn't already?"

"You can be a prick, sometimes."

"Aye, I get that a lot."

"Just leave this alone."

"What do you know about her?"

Susan looked like she was ready to leave. She turned her head to look at a bed of flowers nearby. Rich and vibrant, reds and yellows.

She looked back at me.

"You saw how she died."

"Beaten. Slashed. Shot in the head." I tried to keep my tone professional. Dispassionate. Couldn't stop my stomach turning or a sweat breaking out beneath my shirt.

"What does that tell you?"

"Whoever did it wasn't afraid to get their hands dirty."

"Whoever did this knew what they were doing. They took their time. Kept her alive as long as possible." She took a deep breath, held it for a few seconds. "That last thing, the bullet in the face…"

"Why suspect my client?"

"Motive. Opportunity."

"But no means."

"You're certain?"

"You know something I don't?"

Susan started cracking the knuckles on her left hand. "The only gun on the property was a licensed shotgun. For shooting grouse. He takes the proper precautions."

"A shotgun didn't kill her."

"No. That's the unanswered question if your client is responsible... where did he get the gun that did kill her?"

"Her murder was professional."

"What makes you say that?"

"Instinct. Something about the way the body was left out in the open. Like whoever killed her wanted us to find the corpse."

"Aye, that's it. All we have on Robertson is motive, but... it's enough to make you stop and think."

"You know as well as I do..."

"I'm not saying he's guilty, Steed. Pretty much crossed off the list, in fact. He acts guilty, you know, but even the DI doesn't think he's a murderer..."

"Then who...?"

She seemed to have to gather up the nerve to ask, "Do you know who she is?"

"I don't know much except her name... Kat..."

"Short for Katrina, Steed. Her maiden name was Campbell. But she took the name of her husband. Gordon Egg. "

I thought: *fuck*. Said: "She told me she was Daniel's girlfriend." Came to the logical conclusion. "They were fucking behind Egg's back?"

"Aye, right enough. That's a subtle way with words you have. I'm surprised Lindsay didn't say anything."

"Maybe it slipped his mind."

Or maybe he thought that would have only encouraged me.

"Maybe it did. But you understand what I'm trying to tell you?"

"Loud and clear." This was too big for me to get involved. Something Lindsay had tried to tell me earlier.

"Wish it was that simple," she said. When I asked what she meant, she added, "Believing you."

This was the first time we'd talked properly in months, and here I was using her as a resource. Not a friend. Acting as though all I cared about was what she could tell me. No wonder she'd looked ready to walk away.

So I had to ask myself what it was that had made her stay.

I couldn't answer.

As the sun shifted across the sky, the shadows in the quadrangle fell to new angles. The shadow that was above us had moved slowly, and now the sun shone on Susan's face and she half-closed her eyes so that it wouldn't blind her.

I thought about her face in the moonlight that came through the slats of blinds. About the sound of her breath, the feel of her skin.

"So who killed her? Not the man himself."

"Like we could get it back to him through anything other than supposition." She seemed to think about it, then shook her head. "We just don't know."

"You must have an idea."

"Take your pick."

"Locally, he had ties to Martin Kennedy and his boys in the eighties. But Kennedy Sr's dead."

"And his last remaining son is in prison."

"So that leaves…"

"Aye, David Burns."

"Jesus fuck."

"I've never met him. I've heard Lindsay talk about him."

"I was at his house once."

David Burns. Entrepreneur. In both the legal and illegal senses. An old school hard bastard who made sure the shite never stuck long enough to get him locked up.

"His wife spat in my face. Not for any other reason than I was the first copper she saw."

Susan said, "The thing is… Burns has been playing up his public image recently. The organised crime days are long gone, so he claims. He's legit. Far as a man like him can get. And why would he go around fouling on his own doorstep?"

"Why, indeed."

"Do you understand, Steed, the reasons I'm asking you to back off?"

I understood. Didn't mean I cared for it. Call me stubborn. Susan was probably thinking about calling me much worse.

"How about this? I back off. You keep me up to speed."

I stood up. "The way things are between us, now, I don't owe you an explanation."

Chapter 15

I couldn't sleep.

Lying on top of the bed covers, I turned on the bedside light and watched a spider crawl across the ceiling. A big fellow with a fat body and long legs.

How did he get inside the flat. Where did he live? Where did he think he was going? What was he thinking every time he paused on his journey?

Was he taking stock of his surroundings? Figuring out a plan? Or merely drawing breath?

But he wasn't thinking. He was acting on instinct.

He was thinking after a fashion, of course. But not overdoing it. Not intellectualising or trivialising the reality of his situation.

Realising that made me jealous.

I closed my eyes, tried to empty my mind.

But I kept churning over scenarios and possibilities, still obsessed with a case I should have left behind the moment Robertson scrawled his angry signature on the cheque.

I'd spent seven years on the force. Not a lifetime,

but long enough to know when I was being lied to. And when someone was telling me the truth. Susan knew it, too. And Lindsay.

James Robertson hadn't killed Katrina Egg. He'd thought about it, I was sure. But he hadn't done it.

But if not him, then who?

The attack had been bloody and violent. Malicious. No hesitation. No doubt. It was planned.

Like Susan said: professional.

And yet, enough ferocity that it still felt... personal.

I couldn't leave it alone. Anyone with an ounce of common sense would have backed away long before now, but I had this urge to keep pressing forward. I'd told Susan to keep me updated. Saying, if she did that then I'd leave it alone.

Even that compromise left me itching.

I didn't have all the answers my ex-client had asked for.

Daniel had been on the run. Why else would he come back? Not because of lingering guilt. Certainly not because of any family connections. Look at the reaction to his father's heart attack.

It had been panic. He had nowhere else to turn.

I remembered the voice of the man at the club. His tone had darkened when I mentioned Daniel.

Danny-boy, what did you do?

Was it really something as simple as sleeping with the boss's wife?

But then, she hadn't seemed nervous when she stood in my office. Not in that way. Concerned, perhaps, for Daniel, worried about what he'd done. But surely she would have been as scared of her husband as anyone else. She would have known he was capable of killing her.

I felt like I was close to some revelation, but couldn't quite clear that final hurdle. I tried to sleep, thinking my mind could sort itself out on its own. But it didn't work. I couldn't get still. Couldn't stop thinking.

Everything came back to what Daniel Robertson had done. The thing that got him fired from the club had been what killed him. What fucked up his brother's life. What killed Kat, the woman who had claimed she loved him.

There were answers to all my questions. But I feared they were in the grave.

Chapter 16

At eight o'clock, I awoke to hear my mobile ringing on the bedside table through in the other room. Rolling off the sofa and struggling to my feet, I found I'd fallen asleep the wrong way. My muscles were stiff. The only movements I could coax from them were tentative and uncertain.

Nevertheless, I limped through to the bedroom and took the call.

"I want to talk to you," Robertson said.

"About the report?"

"Face to face. I think I know who killed that woman."

"You should call the police," I said, deferring to common sense. "Talk to DI Lindsay. He'll be able to —"

"I can't... I... Christ, McNee, I don't know if I can talk to the police." He sounded ready to break down in tears. Maybe he already had.

I took a deep breath, thought about what had happened to Kat. The fear in Robertson's voice was transparent. I said, "Okay, we'll talk," and named a café where we could meet.

He hung up without saying goodbye.

I wasn't going back on my word if I talked to him. At the very least I could tell him what Susan had told me. His problems couldn't be solved by private parties. The police weren't out to crucify him, they were out to find the truth.

And I could do nothing else to help him.

My part was over. I wasn't going to get involved.

And I wondered if, like me, he'd find my resolution hollow.

***

The Washington Café on Union Street was small, with green, vinyl-covered pews and plastic tables. It shouldn't have survived past 1950 and as such felt homely and welcoming. Like a time capsule. It was comforting to think that among all the changes that had occurred in the city centre, some places just kept on going.

Robertson had slipped behind a table at the rear. I ordered a black coffee for myself. The wee woman behind the till told me she'd bring it over.

I sat opposite Robertson, who sipped from a mug of milky-white tea. His eyes were supported by bags. I knew how he felt.

His hands shook, in danger of letting his cup slip from between his fingers. I could smell the whisky on his breath.

"You didn't sound good on the phone," I said.

"I had no reason to sound good."

"You've been holding back since our first consultation. There's something else going on."

"No. Nothing else." I would have believed him except his eyes were focused on the plastic table top and his voice trembled despite his best efforts at composure.

"If you know something..."

"Last night I got a phone call." He looked up at me again. Bloodshot eyes made him look like he'd drunk enough booze to re-float the *Titanic*. "A Cockney accent, you know, like that bloody *EastEnders* shite." He sipped from his cup, winced. Then blew on the hot liquid to cool it down. "Asking about my brother."

"You mean his suicide?"

"No. This... this bastard...told me my brother had stolen something."

"Like what?"

"Like money. I don't know how much," Robertson said, and I thought he was a little too quick with that information. "He just said money. That was all. He said I knew where it was."

"You don't know what he was talking about?"

"The first time I saw my brother in over thirty years was when I found him hanging from a tree, Mr McNee."

"This man on the phone, did he say anything else?"

"He said to wait and they'd be in touch."

"Did he threaten you?"

"Are you no listening, you stupid bloody eejit!"

I sat back. Folded my arms. Waited.

Finally: "It wasn't *what* he said."

I nodded. "You should go to the police."

"You said. And tell them what? They've got their hands full looking into that woman's murder. And they suspect me of that, as well. Calling the police isn't going to do any good, McNee."

"So what do you want me to do?"

"Your advert said you do security work. So I want your services on another job. Security."

"Securing you?"

"Aye."

"Like a bodyguard?"

"Aye. Like a bodyguard." Talking slowly, as if I was a child.

I shook my head. "Mr Robertson, you're right. You need protection. But you should go to the police. Hiring private security is all well and fine, but I still recommend that—"

"Whatever," he said. "I'm no going to the police."

I wanted back in. Even if it meant I would be stepping out of my depth.

At the very least, I had to make a gesture of hesitance. I owed Susan that, at least.

"Okay." I pulled out my phone. "I'm going to give you some numbers. Professional security guys, people with experience in this—"

"I don't want them on the job."

"Sure, but I don't have the experience that—"

He stood up. "I'm asking for your help," he said, his voice loud enough that it attracted attention from the other diners. "Because I don't trust anyone else to deal with this. I don't know these people whose numbers you've got on your phone. And I definitely don't trust the police any more than they're going to trust what I tell them." He stepped out from the booth. "Cash the bloody cheque, you parasitic bastard, before I cancel it."

Maybe he expected me to follow him. But I stayed where I was, cupping my coffee between my hands and waiting until I heard him leave.

He was scared, and I couldn't blame him for that.

But his refusal to even think about approaching the police was what intrigued me. Any normal citizen with nothing to hide wouldn't have thought twice about approaching the boys in blue, but Robertson had refused point blank. It wasn't the phone call that had scared him. Something else was preying on his mind.

Chapter 17

They never caught the man who killed Elaine.

They didn't even know if he was a man.

That's the way the world is, sometimes. Resolutions are a long time coming, if they ever come at all. And sometimes you find yourself asking the universe, "why?"

I understood why Martin Barrow blamed me for his daughter's death. In the moments before the accident, we'd been fighting. It had been a stupid fight and I wish she was still around so we could have more of them.

Elaine's father, sitting in the back seat, had been on her side, probably wishing he could just punt me out the door.

If he had, maybe things would have worked out differently.

***

After the accident, they referred me to a psychiatrist.

At first it had been optional. Grief counselling. But

I'd been stubborn and insisted that I was fine. That returning to work was the best way for me to deal with what had happened.

And then I'd broken a DI's nose.

In part because I didn't like the man.

But also because he told me what I already knew, and what I'd already dismissed: they couldn't find the man in the other car.

The doctor who saw me was a tall man with curly hair and Michael Caine glasses. He was skeletally thin and wore cords in an attempt to be ironic. He spoke slowly, with the gentle lilt of Aberdeen hiding somewhere in his words.

"You felt good when you punched the DI?"

This was maybe our second or third session, and I guess he believed that by then we should have made some connection. I should have been comfortable talking to him. He was the kind of man people liked talking to.

Truth was, I thought he was an arrogant prick who'd never known the kind of agony you go through when you lose someone so senselessly. Learned everything in the classroom. Passed his exams with flying colours. Fooled them into thinking he had some kind of empathy with people.

He didn't fool me.

In spite of that, I made an attempt to open up. "Anyone would feel good, breaking that fucker's nose."

"He's not popular?"

"He's not a people person."

The doctor sat in a leather chair with a reclining back. He tucked his left leg up underneath him. Trying to look relaxed. But it was an act. Like everything else about him. If he was a good psychiatrist, he made me think they were all a bunch of con-artists.

"You would say you're a people person?"

"No."

He waited, as though expecting more of a response.

"So you broke his nose because you didn't like him?"

"Why not?"

I kept my eyes fixed on the picture that was framed behind his desk. A black and white picture of the Tay Rail Bridge, shot from underneath. Gulls flitting about the struts. The image was at once majestic and imposing.

"Because he told you something you didn't want to hear."

"I know that's what it looks like." But he'd got something there, this soft talking man with the serious expression.

"But?"

"But… you don't know this bastard. He hates me, always has done."

"And yet he stepped forward to take charge of your case. He wanted to find this other driver…"

"And he didn't."

"You think he failed on purpose?"

"It's possible."

"But unlikely."

He had me over a barrel. I never liked Lindsay and God knew he never liked me. But it didn't make Lindsay a bad guy. Certainly didn't make him the kind of man who'd fuck up an investigation simply for revenge. He was stupid. Petty.

But not malicious.

What I always wondered was why he stepped up to take charge of the inquiry in the first place.

The doctor shifted in his chair. Unfurled his leg. Sat forward. "Do you ever think that you've just been looking for someone to blame?"

"I know that he didn't..."

"People have a basic need. For closure. For resolution. We don't like things to remain unexplained. In your case, you need to find someone to hold responsible for your fiancée's death. You have a need to see justice, or at least to gain some kind of revenge. To look them in the eye and let them see what they did to you."

"But I'll never have that."

"Aye, but it doesn't stop you from trying to find a scapegoat, anyway, does it?"

I attended maybe seven or eight sessions before I finally walked out.

Of everything.

Chapter 18

The book was called *Hard Boiled*. There was a picture of Gordon Egg on the front; a close-up, snarling photo of a man who played his hard-bastard image like a pantomime villain. The picture was maybe five or six years old. The back cover copy was chummy, the author presenting Egg as your charming but slightly dodgy best mate: a misunderstood criminal.

I was sitting on one of the sofas dotted about downstairs in the Waterstone's on Commercial Street. I wasn't ready to buy the book yet, but I was prepared to browse, maybe get a coffee from the Costas upstairs.

Hard Boiled told me nothing: a bog standard biography of a man whose criminal exploits were glorified by the media and subtly approved by the z-list celebrities who frequented his nightclubs.

I read a few more pages, tried to pick up anything I didn't already know from tattle-tale tabloids, but the simplified prose and the implicit acceptance of the man's life and attitudes prevented me from gaining any new insight.

I gave up.

***

"Catching up on your reading, eh, Steed?"

I looked up and saw Constable Susan Bright standing at my table. Dressed in jeans and a black, baggy jumper. Carrying a bottle of overpriced mineral water and a chilled glass. A stray strand of dark hair flopped across the front of her face.

I gestured towards the seat across from me. She sat down in it after only a moment's hesitation. Unscrewed the lid on her water and poured it into the glass. Took a sip before looking at me with those sharp, blue eyes.

"Is it a coincidence?" I asked. "Your being here?"

"Aye, right enough," she said. "You never told me... when you left on compassionate grounds. You really just walked away?"

"Or was I pushed?"

"You were left pushing paper. Not what you signed on for, yeah? And definitely not the kind of work I could see you doing the rest of your life."

"You mean sitting down? For even a minute?"

"Aye, that's it exactly. And what you did to DI Lindsay in the canteen... I think everyone who's ever met him wanted to do that. And it was understandable, maybe, given what happened to you... but..." She stopped talking, looked across at me as though she could somehow see the answer written behind my eyes.

I shifted my gaze.

"We need to find your client," she said. "He's gone

missing."

"I told you I wasn't involved... and besides, he chucked me. I don't go where I'm not wanted."

It was shite and she knew it.

"He really tried, you know."

"I'm sorry?"

"DI Lindsay. When he took over the inquiry. He really tried to find the driver of the other car."

"I don't doubt it."

"Say it like you mean it."

I shrugged.

"The two of you are as bad as each other."

"He sent you here?"

"No. I just... he asked me to have a word with you. He said he had better things to do than listen to you bullshit him the whole time."

"So he sent you down instead. Thoughtful. You must have pissed him off yourself."

She swallowed hard, looked ready to slap me. Then: "If you're hiding something from us — impeding the investigation — Lindsay won't hesitate to smack you down." Her voice low and controlled.

"Maybe he'll just send you to do it instead."

"Do you want to tell me what I did to you?"

Worse than the slap her expression had threatened.

She took a breath, carried on like she hadn't said anything. "We're offering you a chance to co-operate with the investigation, McNee. Do you understand that? This is your way into this. You said you wanted to see it through."

"When you say I'll be in, you mean that I'll get told what happened when everything is done and that if I want to talk to anyone, I'll have to leave a fucking message on someone's answer phone and hope that some fucker gets back to me."

She swigged her water.

"Fuck you," she said, eloquently.

I thought of a time when we'd been open with each other. Friends, and then something else, and then... this.

Everything I had done since Elaine's death looked like a deliberate attempt to isolate myself from people who cared, and perhaps even more people who didn't.

I looked intently at my coffee, waited until she had walked past me before I looked up. My heart beat hard in my chest. When she was gone, I knocked over the coffee, watched the liquid spill over the side of the table and onto the floor. The mug shattered. People looked across. I stood up walked out.

I caught the eye of an old lady. She watched me closely, as though worried I might attack her. I shrugged as I passed her. Said, "I'm sick of coffee."

Chapter 19

When I got back to the office, I called a solicitor I sometimes worked for, asked him if he could get me the name of a landlord from the property address. I gave him the address of the flat on Park Place where Kat was killed. Waited for him to call back.

I already knew who owned the place. I just wanted it verified.

When the solicitor called back, he told me the flat belonged to Burns Property. I thanked him for his time and hung up before I had to make small talk.

The police had to know by now. It wasn't enough to warrant Burns's arrest, but it was a clear indicator of his involvement.

David Burns was either getting sloppy in his old age, or someone had fucked up.

The police should have found another body by now. Some low-life waster; beaten and dumped unceremoniously in a council wheelybin. The guilty party. The Judas. Scapegoat. Whatever.

Susan was right: this was way beyond me. The

police, if they ever made the connection, would probably never find Katrina Egg's killer. Her husband had to be in on the murder. Burns wouldn't risk starting a war with a man like Egg, even if the bastard was based several hundred miles away.

These days, London and Dundee weren't as far apart as they used to be.

But I needed someone to blame. So what could I do? Go to Burns's house, knock on the door and ask for the name and address of the murderer?

I'd end up dead myself.

Someone battered on my office door. Not Bill. The sound was too heavy.

"Open up, you cunt!"

A Cockney accent. Deep, harsh.

"Fuckin' open up."

I thought about Bill out in reception.

I opened the door, stood back.

The man outside was tall, with dark hair cut short in a near-military style. He didn't stand like a soldier, however. More like a thug in dark-blue jeans and a black jumper. He wore a leather bomber-jacket and held a handgun.

He smiled. "You must be McNee."

I kept quiet.

"Seen your card. Friend of ours tried to give it us. Think we must have dropped it in her flat, maybe."

"Yeah," said another voice. "On the rug."

The second speaker was standing by Bill's desk, a double-barrelled shotgun trained on Bill. He was shorter than his companion, barrel-chested and bald. He wore a long coat that swept down to his ankles and, underneath that, black jeans and a white shirt. A scar ran down his left cheek.

"You're not with the police?" I asked.

The taller thug swung his gun arm. Cracked me across the face. I felt the weight of the gun against my jaw, and, as the pain sharpened, my stomach started to heave. I rolled with the blow and steadied myself against the doorframe.

The pain in my jaw stayed there, buzzing.

I swallowed, tasted blood.

Blinked. Got my vision back into focus.

"Smart cunt, ain't you?" The taller thug smiled. Nothing pleasant about it. "My name's Mathew Ayer. My partner there is Richard Liman."

"Doesn't mean anything to me."

"Just being polite." Turning, like he had nothing to worry about. Ayer said to his friend, "These fucking Scottish pricks, eh?"

"Tell me about it."

No point playing games with these two. "You work for Gordon Egg."

"Thought you hadn't heard of us?" Ayer's head snapped back towards me.

"I'm not as dumb as I look."

"Pretty smart for a tartan cunt," Ayer conceded. "Why don't you come out here, say hello to your friend."

Ayer grabbed my shoulder, forced me out into reception. I didn't resist.

I looked at Bill. He tried for a smile. A good effort, but his face was pale and his eyes were wide, his gaze flickering, like he was looking for some kind of escape.

"This fella looks like a queer," said Liman, nodding towards Bill.

To me, Ayer said, "That right? You two bum buddies? A real man would have a hot blonde number for a secretary, right?"

I kept quiet.

Bill did likewise.

"Yeah, I reckon that's what it is," said Ayer. "Playing at PIs. You wear a fucking trenchcoat and a hat while you fuck him?"

"I just had fucking lunch," Liman moaned.

Ayer laughed. "Not like there's nothing wrong with it. It's a free country and all. You two do what you want to each other." He looked at Liman. "Bigoted fuck," he said. "Get with the times."

"Don't mean being a poof is right."

"You'll have to excuse my friend here. Last time inside, I think someone fucking did something turned him against your sort, know what I mean?"

My jaw throbbed. My vision kept blurring.

"Danny was a mate of mine," Ayer said, conversationally. "You knew him?"

"No."

"But you know his brother?"

I shrugged. He smashed me with the gun again. I went down on my knees.

Everything went out of focus.

I rolled onto my back.

Ayer became a shapeless blob. I liked him better that way.

"Give you a fuckin' concussion, mate," he said. "If you keep that up."

Liman laughed. No, he giggled. Like a child.

"You know Danny's brother," Ayer said again. "The fat fuckin' farmer. So don't try to say anything. She told us everything before she died."

Liman giggled again.

"We went to have a word with him today. Took a bit of work to get a fuckin' address, you see. Else we might have been out of this fucking armpit of a country a lot sooner. As it is, the cunt's done a vanishing act. Figured you'd know how to get in touch with him."

He gave me a moment to reply.

I gave him nothing.

"Else you'd know where the fuckin' money was."

The phone call Robertson had received.

"I don't know anything about any money. Neither does my client."

Liman said, "These fuckin' Scottish arseholes, Matt, they don't exactly fuckin' share the wealth. Tight bastards."

"Yeah, I've heard that, too," Ayer agreed. "It's what made England great, you know. Never have had a fuckin' hero like Robin Hood up here in Jock Land."

"Keep his fucking money in his tights, he would."

"Yeah." Looking at me, now. "Wouldn't you say?"

I wanted to tell him where he could go. I wanted to say a thousand things. I wanted to pick myself up off the floor and punch his fucking lights out.

But I stayed where I was. Said nothing. Did nothing. I wasn't stupid.

"So tell me," said Ayer, "about the fucking farmer."

"I don't know where he is."

Ayer took two steps forward, and bent down. He wrapped one large hand around my throat, pulled me up. I went with him. Didn't have a choice. He pushed me against the wall.

Squeezed.

Tears leaked from my eyes.

Blood vessels throbbed in my temples.

"You saw what we did to that bitch."

"I don't fucking know." He had to understand that I didn't have the information he wanted.

114

He let go of my throat.

I collapsed to the floor, coughing as I struggled to get the air back into my lungs. My chest felt like it was being stabbed from the inside.

"He doesn't fucking know," Ayer said.

"No?"

"Fuck all we can do that about that."

Liman tucked his shotgun away beneath the long coat. "Pity, that."

"Yeah, real shame. All you can do is ask, eh?"

I stayed on the floor, watching as they made to leave.

Ayer said, "You know, I can never tell when a man is lying. So how about we call this a gentle fucking reminder of what happens if I find out you haven't been telling the truth."

And, casually, as he walked out the door, he shot Bill in the stomach.

Chapter 20

I thought for a moment that the noise of the gunshot had blown out my eardrums.

Bill fell back, smashed off the desk, thumped onto the floor.

When I looked up, Ayer and Liman were gone.

I tried to move, but my body had shut down. I was going nowhere.

Fuck that.

I forced myself onto my feet. Slowly.

Moved over to Bill. He was on the floor, behind his desk. Legs tangled up in the toppled chair.

Blood leaked onto the wooden boards. Already, he'd lost too much.

He looked at me with wide eyes and said, "I thought it would hurt more."

"Hold on," I said. Grabbed the phone off the desk.

The woman on the other end told me to remain calm. She sounded like somebody's mother. Comforting. Authoritative. I told her a man had been shot, and I was doing pretty well considering the circumstances.

An ambulance would be with me shortly. The police had been informed.

The office was two minutes walk from FHQ. I knew who'd get here first.

She asked me to stay on the line but I told her I couldn't. After hanging up, I tried to move Bill into the recovery position.

I just had to touch him and he screamed.

"If I stay still," he told me, "it's fine."

Sure.

"Look at me," I told him. "Just keep your eyes on me."

"Do you know what you're doing?"

"Fuck, no," I said. I knew basic first aid, but the last thing I expected to see in my office was a man shot in the gut.

"There's a surprise, man." He giggled. Blood pumped faster.

I grabbed Bill's jacket from where it was slung in the cupboard that laughingly passed for a cloakroom. I bundled it over the wound, pressed hard.

"Fucking hell!"

"You'll bleed out," I said. "I don't want you dead."

"Funny way of showing it." Speaking slower, now, his words slurring. His eyeballs rolled.

"I'd rather hurt you than watch you die." He smiled at that, but I could see he was getting away from me. "Fucking stay awake," I said. He wasn't dying. Not if I could do something.

Not this time.

* * *

"Look at this fucking prick! There's your criminal right there."

117

I remember thinking I should never have walked in. I should have stayed out of the way. But I couldn't help myself.

Lindsay started to stand up, his eyes fixed on mine.

I ignored him.

"Martin," I said, with no idea of how I was going to continue.

"Fuck you." Elaine's father stood up. His chair scraped backwards across the floor.

We needed to talk. If he would just listen, maybe we could reach a kind of understanding.

But instead of saying anything, all I did was clear my throat.

Lindsay said, "This couldn't wait?" He'd already turned off the tape recorder. This confrontation was never going on the record.

Martin Barrow was a tall man, with a sinewy body and muscles like thick rope. He had been bald since his late thirties, and his prominent nose gave him an almost regal appearance.

He walked round the desk.

Lindsay stood between us. "Mr Barrow, please sit down."

I tried to say something. "I just wanted to —"

Elaine's father made to rush me. The tendons in his neck stood out. His eyes bulged. His skin darkened with rage.

Lindsay held him back. Looking at me. "Get the fuck out of here."

Martin Barrow kept trying to force his way past the other man. "He knows it, too. He knows what he did. The fucking coward. Can't even face up to his own responsibility." Then, perfectly still, his eyes on

118

me: "This was your fucking fault."

How could I argue with that?

***

"Follow my finger."

"I'm fine."

"Follow the finger." The doctor wagged a digit in front of my face. I followed it as best I could. She nodded, apparently satisfied. "No concussion."

"I could have told you that."

She sighed, and folded her arms across her chest. "You were lucky. From the sound of it, anyway." She was a tall woman with curly dark hair and a strong Mancunian accent. And an expression that told me she wasn't going to take any shite. Not from me. Not from anyone.

"How's Bill doing?"

"The man who came in with you? I don't know."

She turned away. There was a sink on the wall behind the bed. She scrubbed her hands there.

"I could find out," she said.

"I'd feel better if you could."

"That's something, I suppose."

I tried to stand up. She watched me and said, "You didn't mention any discomfort in your leg."

"Old injury."

"Really?"

"Aye."

"We should take a look at it."

"It's been looked at. Nothing doing."

"How long ago?"

"Long enough."

"It could be worth another examination. They might have overlooked something the first time round. Or

119

you've developed something since…."

"No, its fine."

The Mancunian doctor told me to lie back down on the bed again and wait for someone to come and have a word with me.

"You said I was okay."

"Wait," she said.

I lay back down on the bed, let my head sink into the pillow. I stayed like that until she was gone. Then I swung my legs over the end of the bed.

I moved out from behind the curtains and limped through A&E. My calf muscles screamed in protest.

A nurse confronted me. A short woman who could have been any age between twenty and forty. I doubted she ever smiled. Didn't have the features for it. "Can I help you?" Nothing helpful in her tone, either.

"I'm looking for a friend."

"Visiting hours are—"

"I know," I said. "He was brought in here maybe half an hour ago. Gunshot wound…"

She nodded. "I heard about that. Unusual for the Dee, eh?"

I agreed with her.

She looked almost ready to let me go, and then: "You came in with him. With the police."

"Yes."

"You shouldn't be walking about."

"I just need to know that my friend is…"

She pointed back the way I had come. "I don't have time for this. None of us do. It's not just you and your friend… we've got all the usual bloody headaches to deal with, too."

"It's okay," said a voice from behind me. "We'll have a word with him."

Lindsay nodded in greeting when I turned to face him.

"How is he?"

"Your wee pal? He'll live."

"Good."

"I don't know about you, but I could do with some fresh air."

The nurse said, "I'm not sure that it's safe for the patient to—"

"Oh, he looks fine to me," said Lindsay. "I'm no doctor, of course." His own joke provoked a genuine smile.

I guess someone had to find him funny.

***

Outside, we looked to the west of the city. From the A&E entrance we could see all the way down to the Kingsway. Car lights slipped through the dark.

"It was touch and go," said Lindsay, "when they got him in."

"But he's fine?"

"He'll live." He sparked up a cigarette. "Like I said."

"But?"

"He might be paralysed."

"Fuck."

Lindsay took a puff on the cigarette, then turned to look at me. "That's one reaction." Here we were again. Someone's life thrown in the shitter and it all came back to me.

I could look for someone else to blame, but here was the truth: I was the one who had put him in the position where those bastards could shoot him.

Lindsay offered me a cigarette. Nothing friendly in

the gesture.

"I don't smoke."

"You did when you joined the force."

The first time we ever met: the now defunct smokers' lounge in FHQ. Even then, our relationship could only have been described as hostile.

Love at first sight?

In this case, try "loathing".

"I got health conscious."

"Self-righteous prick." The insult was slung half-heartedly.

"You wanted to talk."

"That's right. Because I think you're full of shite." He shivered as he blew out smoke. "When you say you don't know why these pricks shot your friend, I don't believe a word of it."

"I told you everything I know."

"Everything?"

Not quite. "Yes."

"When you don't like someone, you start to lie to them instinctively. I know how it is. There was an old DI... Buchan, that was the bastard's name... Jesus, can't even remember his first name... Adam, maybe? Alex? Who cares, right? He used to tell me I would never make it. Told me I had to be willing to bend a few rules here and there to uphold the principles of being a copper. Don't get me wrong, he wasn't bent, he was just... flexible. And a stubborn shite with it. When I joined CID, some smart prick thought it would be funny to put us together. We had the worst fucking history of anyone in the division because we started lying to each other. Each one trying to fuck the other over. For shits and giggles. Or just because we didn't like each other's faces. Fucking disaster."

He blew out more smoke, watched it drift in the

air. Waited, as though expecting me to say something.

I pretended I hadn't been listening.

"Fine," said Lindsay. "Sulk like a fucking child, see if I care. But get this, pal: I know you're kidding me on. You know something, and this keeping shit to yourself won't do anyone any good." He dropped the cigarette, stubbed it out with his toe. "Least of all that poor prick in surgery."

Chapter 21

Back inside, I saw Andy, Bill's boyfriend, in the A&E
waiting room. He was a tall, gaunt architect with
Jarvis Cocker glasses that magnified his serious eyes.
He was pacing back and forth across the room.
Restless. Pent up energy waiting to find release.

I saw myself, one year earlier.

The memory made me want to turn round and get
the hell out. But I forced myself to stay.

When he saw me, Andy quit stalking and his lips
pressed tight together. He turned his head to the
side.

"Andy," I said. But didn't know how to continue.

"I don't want to talk to you."

"I understand," I said. "But…"

"Listen," he said. "Billy's in fucking surgery and I
don't know if he'll walk again. The one thing I'm
sure of is that all of this is your fault. Playing at
being a fucking private eye."

"I'm not playing."

"Like that makes it better?"

There was nothing I could say to him. All I could do was hope that when this was over he would understand that all of this was outside of my control.

When this was over. When Bill was walking. When everything was normal again.

Except normal seemed a long way away.

I clammed up on Andy, backed out of saying everything I wanted to say.

And walked out.

***

I found an empty stairwell, sat down at the top of a flight and placed my head in my hands. My body shuddered uncontrollably. The anger and frustration tried to shake itself out of me. But it wasn't enough. I wanted to scream. Break some bastard's neck. Anything. Just find a release.

All I could do was feel my insides boil and my brain smash against the inside of my skull in frustration.

Andy was right. Elaine's father was right. Fucking Lindsay was right.

All of them, on the nose.

I was responsible.

Me.

Alone.

"Fuckers!" I screamed it out in the stairwell.

Was I looking for someone to blame? Someone to take it all out on? Aye, well who better than those two pricks. The ones who had violated my fucking life. Near killed my friend.

Murdered a woman in cold blood.

Maybe they thought they were hard men. But their actions reminded me of the cowardice of the school-yard bully.

I could find them. They had unfinished business, these fucking cowards. They wouldn't leave until they had completed their master's bidding.

Daniel Robertson was dead, beyond their reach. Katrina Egg's betrayal had been dealt with. But the money, as far as they were concerned, was still out there. They wouldn't leave without that. Gordon Egg, the greedy prick, wouldn't allow it.

I stood up. Fire in the back of my legs. My muscles protesting, threatening to knock me back down on my arse. I ignored them, walked down the stairs to the ground level of the hospital. Each step deliberate, measured, as I kept that anger inside me, bubbling gently. I would need it, I knew.

A small voice in my head whispered, *this isn't about justice or friendship or compassion: this is about making you feel better.*

But I didn't listen.

Or care.

Chapter 22

I didn't sleep well that night. I sat in the front room of my flat, listening to the sounds of the city; the rush of cars down the street outside, the shouts of drunken pub crawlers a few streets away and the occasional squeal of fire engines and police cars.

It had been around half ten when I got home. I was trying to work out what my next move should be.

That morning, I'd told Robertson: *go to the police*. Advice given half-heartedly, as though I had already known the path that was before me.

Shortly after I got through the door my mobile rang. I checked the number: withheld.

"You back home, then?"

Ayer.

I stood up. Involuntary. "What the fuck is it to you?"

He laughed. "How's the poof?"

"Alive."

"I'm glad." He paused, then: "No, really. Fucking glad. Because that was a warning, yeah?"

"A warning?"

"That's right. In our line of business people don't listen if you just use fuckin' harsh words. They got to know you mean business."

"I would have listened."

"Didn't want to take the chance." I could picture him smirking on the other end of the line.

But I was only half listening. Straining to hear background noises: anything that might give me a clue where he was calling from.

"You talked to the farmer?" he asked.

"It slipped my mind."

That gave him another laugh. I imagined his body before me, battered and broken.

Kept myself focused on that image.

"Good one, mate. Fuckin' good one. Awright, guess you got a point. Gotta make sure the little poof's doing fine, yeah? Well, you know the cunt's going to live so now you can find that fat fuck and tell him we want our fuckin' money."

"Find him yourself."

"He isn't answering his phone no more. Doesn't want to talk to us. Shame, really. He gives us what we want and we just go away. Nothing fuckin' magic about it, yeah? I've had enough of this fuckin' place to last me a lifetime." I thought he was going to hang up, but he wasn't finished. "You tell the fat fuck that he'd better talk to us the next time we call. Tell him he'd better give us what we want. You think what happened to that poof in your office was bad, it ain't nothing. We was gentle with him, mate. Like fuckin' pussy cats. I hope you got the message this time. Because next time isn't no fuckin' warning."

He cleared the line. I listened to the silence for a moment before hanging up. In the living room, I sat in the dark and waited.

It got light around four o'clock. I was still in the chair. Finally, I began to move. I showered, shaved, got dressed.

Replayed the conversation from the night before in my head.

These Cockney bastards were professionals. If Egg had sent them up here, then he trusted them. And if Egg trusted them, they meant business.

Next time isn't no fuckin' warning.

When Robertson had told me about the first phone call, I'd dismissed his fear out of hand. An over-reaction. Natural enough, given everything he'd gone through.

But now I was beginning to understand what these arseholes were capable of.

They weren't just going to give up and go home if we gave them the run around. And they wouldn't give a shite if they knew the coppers were after them. They'd killed Katrina Egg. Shot Bill. Enjoyed it, too. And now they were coming after me and James Robertson.

For these psycho-fucks, reclaiming the big man's missing cash was little more than an afterthought.

Chapter 23

I always thought a city was a place you could lose yourself.

Dundee calls itself a city, but it's hard to become lost here. Elaine, whose family came from Glasgow, called it a small town with pretensions. I guess she was right. Once you've lived here long enough, some days it seems you can't walk ten steps without seeing someone you know.

Which made my staying in the city a perversity of sorts.

Every street dredged up memories of Elaine. The sight of the Law Hill rising above the buildings made me think of when we used to take walks together up the gentle slope towards the observatory.

Was I simply reluctant to let go?

Or was it something more troubling?

The morning after the two Cockney pricks had broken into my office, I found myself walking past Elaine's old flat. It was to the east of the city, situated above a bookies. The gamblers had used her close as an unofficial urinal. The first time she invited me back, she warned me about the smell.

I stood on the street outside, looked up at the window of the third floor flat and imagined I could see her there, looking out the window, waiting for me, translucent, a ghost waiting for a day that would never arrive.

The day she moved out, I remember she took one last look at the hallway before closing the door and following me down the steps and onto the street. I asked her why she looked so sad. She smiled at me and said, "If you live somewhere long enough, you leave a part of yourself there. I was saying good-bye."

I saw movement up there at the window where I imagined her to be standing. And I thought that it was a beautiful idea, leaving part of yourself behind.

But I knew it was bullshit.

***

When Lindsay answered the phone, he sounded irritated. I said, "You wanted to talk. So let's talk."

I told him I'd be there in twenty minutes.

He told me he'd chuck me in the cells for wasting police time.

***

Lindsay stood on the steps out the front of HQ at the West Marketgait entrance. He was smoking a cigarette. His gaze was fixed on the Marketgait, watching the twin lanes of traffic as they swept past. Across the way, empty jute mills had been rejuvenated; student accommodation. The town was

131

transforming; from industry to education and innovation.

"So what do you want to talk about?"

"You were right," I said.

He raised his eyebrows. Forced the grin back off his face. "Really?"

"I'm a stubborn prick. I'm holding shit back because I don't like you. And because of that, people have ended up dead and a man who doesn't deserve it could be a cripple for life."

"Have you called the hospital?"

"No."

"Some friend you are."

"Can we leave this alone?"

"You haven't been looking well lately. When you saw that body, I thought you were about to fall over."

I put weight on my left leg as though to make the point. "I'm doing fine."

He looked like he didn't believe me. But instead of passing comment, he took another puff on his cigarette. He couldn't have looked like he wanted to be here any less.

"These men think I have something that belongs to them," I said. "I don't. Neither does my client."

"Aye? You sure about that?" He took a deep drag on the cigarette. "Your client, the man, Robertson, that's his name? Maybe you can tell me where he is?"

"I don't know," I said, thinking that everyone seemed desperate to find him. "You might want to try him at his home."

He nodded. "Trouble with that is he's no got a home any more. Last night, there was a fire. A monster from what I hear. Black smoke choking up the skies, flames that could singe the back of your eyeballs if you just looked at them. The whole place burnt to ashes. Nothing left." I knew he could see my reaction out of the corner of his eye. "I don't know if there was anyone in there. They're still going through the wreckage. I'm waiting to hear for sure whether it was an accident. I mean, that kind of fire, it's got to be an accident. Unless someone wanted to prove a serious point." He didn't believe that it was an accident. You could hear it in his voice. See it in his face.

I hadn't come here to play games with him. "I have a few ideas."

"No doubt."

"The two men are associates of Gordon Egg."

"I figured."

"Daniel Robertson was having an affair with the big man's wife."

"That's why they killed him?"

"No. They didn't know he was here."

Lindsay nodded. "So we're back to the suicide. Backing up the coroner, eh?"

"Aye. But it still doesn't make sense."

"No?"

"Because he didn't just steal Egg's wife. He stole the man's money, too."

"A final fuck-you, then. This was all about getting back at the big man."

"Maybe, but..."

"But give me something better." I didn't know if he wanted me to shut up, or if he was asking for help.

I looked at him. He stood there, completely confident. Puffing on his cigarette and watching me like I was a suspect in the interrogation room.

I'd come to ask for help and he'd dismissed everything I said. He didn't want to listen. Just wanted to hear me admit that he was right. Getting nothing more out of it than a cheap victory.

I turned to walk away.

Behind me, I heard Lindsay say, "In case you've forgotten, I'm no the bad guy in all of this. Jesus fuckin' Christ, you called me!"

I pretended I couldn't hear him.

***

On Ward Road, I dialled Robertson's mobile number. I was about to give up when he finally answered: "You alone?"

"Aye. You want to tell me about the fire?"

"Do you still think it's a good idea to go to the police?"

"I don't know if you understand the kind of shite your brother got himself mixed up with," I said. "That cash, he stole it from Gordon Egg."

"That's got nothing to do with me."

"They came to my office," I said. "They seem to think you and I are in cahoots. If you know something more than you've already admitted, you need to tell me now."

"I didn't ask for this," he said.

I agreed to meet him. We were in this together, now.

After he cleared the line, I gripped the phone tightly in my hand.

Thought about Gordon Egg. His associates.

I had one chance to make this go away.

And if it was to work, I knew I'd be making a deal with the devil.

But at least this devil was one I knew.

Chapter 24

David Burns came to the front door wearing a thick, dark dressing gown and tartan slippers. He didn't look happy to receive company, even less so when he saw my face.

"I know you," he said. "You've been here before."

I was impressed by his memory. Four years previously, when I was still on the force, someone had tipped off CID regarding Burns' involvement in less than legal pornography designed for those of a more animal bent. We'd come round, all official, knocking politely on the door. He'd invited us in like he and the investigating officer were old friends, but with a cold edge to his manner. Even if he was used to these interruptions, he was hardly going to supply us with cups of tea while chatting about the weather.

The DI in charge had talked to Burns with a familiarity that implied a long relationship. This was fairly close to the truth. Back in the mid eighties, as the police upped their campaign to deal with organised crime in Scotland, men like Burns had signed deals with the authorities to guarantee some level of protection. These backroom deals were complicated, messy and would eventually prove more trouble than they were worth. All the men like Burns would continue to believe they were not viable targets for the coppers even after the initiative was abandoned and forgotten by the chiefs. Small wonder the old man had been unhappy at our unannounced presence that morning. The DI, despite his outward chumminess towards Burns, seemed to take a delight in our host's discomfort and agitation. It was only later that I would discover that he was the same man who had dealt with Burns back in the eighties.

The man who had grudgingly invited us into his home a few years previously had possessed a full head of shocking white hair. These days, he sported a buzz cut to hide a losing battle with baldness, and a great deal of the bulk he'd carried was gone. Despite that, he still looked as though he could snap me in two. And the ice-blue eyes were every bit as penetrating as I remembered.

Sweat stuck my shirt against my spine.

"So," he said, plunging his hands deep into the pockets of his thick dressing-gown, "you got a promotion? You're plainclothes now? You were just a wee uniform back then. Tell me, are you still busting innocent bastards for trumped up charges of perversion?"

I shook my head. "You were never charged."

"What a waste of a morning. For all of us."

"I'm no longer with the police." I reached into my pocket, pulled out my wallet and produced my Association of British Investigators' ID. He grabbed the card. Examined it carefully, his expression dispassionate.

"Must be a fucking pain, having a code of ethics in your line of work."

"We'll get used to it."

"Some of yous, maybe."

"Certain individuals had tainted the profession." Quoting the party line verbatim.

"You'll no be one of them?"

"I like to think not."

"Right. They're calling you Britain's second police force these days?"

"Sure. That's it."

He smiled. "Which makes you a bunch of pricks in anyone's eyes. A bunch of pricks without uniforms."

I ignored him.

"So did they tell you to sling your arse? Or did you just walk? Out of the force, I mean."

I stayed silent.

Burns grinned. I guess he didn't mind deciding on his own version of the truth.

"I was about to have some coffee," he said. "So why don't you come in and I'll see if I like what you have to say for yourself."

I thought about earlier, in the bookshop. Said, "Actually, do you have any tea?"

"All out. The wife didn't get to the shops today."

Inside, the house was decorated in a muted, yet homely style. Dark wood panelling, paintings on the walls. Mostly West Coast scenes: dark and stormy ocean panoramas and craggy mountainsides. There had been a great deal of work done on the house through the years and the money showed subtly throughout.

The kitchen gleamed like new. Designed by someone who knew just how much money the customer had to spend. It was not a practical kitchen, but a statement of wealth and property. Burns had come a long way from his formative years when he had been stuck in the darkest Dundonian tenements, relying on petty crime to sustain him and his family.

But the same bitterness that drove him then still fuelled his actions. Even if he had achieved everything he wanted and more.

He gestured for me to take a seat at the breakfast bar while he trekked to the far end of the kitchen and filled the kettle. He turned back to face me, leaning against the worktop. Deceptively casual. "You can start talking."

"About two weeks ago, a man committed suicide. Hung himself from a tree out in the Tentsmuir woods. His name was Daniel Robertson."

"I read the papers, son. What's that to do with me?"

"Robertson worked for an associate of yours: Gordon Egg. A few days ago, Katrina Egg — his wife — came to Dundee looking for Daniel. She didn't seem to know he was dead, was anxious to get a hold of him."

"If I remember correctly, Egg had a wee Scottish pal he was close to. Friend of the family and all that. I guess maybe he's the same lad. She could have just been worried. Trying to find out what happened to him."

"Sure," I said. "It's a possibility. And maybe I'd think so too. Except, she turned up dead within a couple of days."

"That's a shame."

"Aye, it is. Murdered, you see."

"Christ." No emotion in his voice. All the focus in his eyes trained on me. Like he could see through my skull, make out the thoughts in my brain.

"There are details that won't make the papers."

"Sounds bad."

"It was. Somebody had it in for her."

"Aye. Or her husband."

"Sure. It could be that."

"But considering who her husband is and why she was here…"

"Sure, there's that, too."

Burns nodded thoughtfully. He turned as the kettle clicked, calmly started distributing instant coffee into two mugs. "I hope you don't mind it black," he said. "Like I said about the wife…."

I waited for him to bring the mugs over, took the one he offered. Kept my eyes on him as he sat himself down two seats away from me on the breakfast bar. He blew on the surface of his coffee, his face neutral, his body language casual, like I hadn't just told him about a woman being brutally assaulted and killed in cold blood.

Death could not shake this man. Not after all he had seen and done.

Rumours and stories. Such as: a local priest with a gambling habit. In debt and presumably abandoned by the Lord, the priest had tried to run out on the men he owed. Burns, at the behest of one of the debtors, tracked down this man of the cloth and arranged an alternative payment. The priest was found in his church, nailed to the cross at the rear of the pulpit. Proper job, too. Through the wrists rather than the palms. A claw hammer had been left at his feet, in order that someone could prise the nails free and let him down.

Never let it be said David Burns didn't have some sense of mercy.

He was older, now, but he had not allowed the

years to soften him.

You looked in his eyes and you could still see the storm raging there. You wondered: what was it that had made him so angry? What makes a man like this keep going?

"The obvious suspect is Daniel's estranged brother," I said, trying not to back down under Burns's gaze. "He had already been trying to dig up the facts on his brother's life. He wasn't going to be too happy to learn that his brother had been a heavy with some London firm."

"And where do you come into all of this?"

I ignored him. "I don't think that Daniel's brother was responsible for Katrina Egg's death. There's the question of how her body got in the flat. I believe the property belongs to you, right?"

He sipped calmly at his coffee. He had nothing to worry about. Yet.

"I was questioned about this the other day," he said. "A police detective by the name of George Lindsay. You know him? I'll tell you what I told the police: I just rent that place out. What goes on inside, I can't be held responsible for that."

"Aye, so maybe they broke in," I said. "And that should have been an end to it all. A sad and unfortunate end, perhaps. But an end."

"I still don't get," said Burns, "how you've got this coming back to me. Except by rumour and conjecture. I don't know how these bastards got into my flat. Which was, incidentally, unoccupied at the time." He seemed to take a moment to think about that before adding, "To the best of my knowledge. So I don't see how I can help you, son." Putting emphasis on the "son", like it was an insult. "And again, I ask, what the fuck does any of this have to do with you?"

"I represent Daniel's brother. When he wanted to know more about who his brother had become, he came to me."

"So it's really a step up from being copper? Muckraking, I mean?" He watched me for any reaction.

I gave him nothing.

"Tell me, was he happy when you found out? About who his brother was? The kind of people he associated with?"

"People like you?"

For a second, I thought I'd touched a nerve. His eyes twitched. Barely noticeable, but it was there.

And then he laughed.

"Very good," he said. "Are you sure you're not still a copper?"

"I'm sure." I sipped at my coffee.

"You didn't know Kat. She was a fucking black widow spider. She chewed men up and spat them out. It was a game to her, fucking all these hard men and then watching her husband do them over when he found out."

"He never touched her?"

"No. She was perfect. In his eyes, at least. All these men she shagged, they were the ones who corrupted her."

I thought about the woman who had walked into my office. Trying so hard to be attractive. Dolled up. Trying to retain the illusion of sexuality.

And I thought about the hardness I had seen behind her eyes. Realised there had been a cruelty there, too. Something I should have seen.

And I had to wonder whether my refusal to see that side of her hadn't been deliberate.

"So I say good riddance to her," Burns said. "Maybe she didn't deserve to go like that, but a person can only push their luck so long, eh?"

I felt sick.

Said, "You keep asking what any of this has to do with me. It goes beyond my client, now. Last night I had a couple of visitors. Cockney hard bastards. They threatened me. They shot my friend."

"I'm sorry." My own words, my mantra, echoed back at me. With no conviction.

"He'll live." And, I thought, not that you care. "They said it was a warning."

"I'm sorry about your friend. And I'm sorry about your... situation. But I don't know why you're here."

"You knew Egg. Maybe you know where these men are. Maybe you can talk to them. Tell them that I don't know anything. That my client doesn't know anything."

"Even if I knew where they were, why should I care?"

"Because Dundee's your city. You're proud to be a native son. A man who chose to stay here. Make his life here. And then these bastards come up, start spilling blood on your streets and in your property. You said the police were talking to you, and I know that you're a respectable businessman these days. So that has to sting a little, to know these pricks are jeopardising your good name."

Burns blew on his coffee. I saw the ripples over the lip of the mug, thought of the Tay on the darkest of nights, hiding secrets in its depths. "If I knew these pricks," he said. "Maybe I'd have a word with them." He set down his mug on the table. "But these days, as you said, I'm nothing more than a businessman. A humble landlord. I rent flats, I have a hand in a few pubs. All above board. I live a simpler life these days. I made my money. Paid the bloody piper. And now I just want to live here in peace. With my family. My wife. My daughter and her new husband down the street. Grandchildren coming round to see the old man. Hoping I'll have sweeties hidden in a drawer for them. Knowing I've got them. The past is the past, Mr McNee. Now I'm just a family man."

Warmed over shite. Burns was still hip deep in illegal activities. All that had changed was he had become the man giving the orders instead of taking them. He had amassed a degree of deniability.

I stood up. "Think about it," I said. "You told me that Egg loved his wife. That he never blamed her before no matter who she slept with. But if she's dead on his say-so, then you know that there's going to be more blood spilt up here. And the way these fucks seem to operate, it's all going to be on your doorstep."

Burns smiled, cocky and confident. "That is if your wee cock and bull theory is anywhere near the truth," he said. "And if these hard cunts know my friend. And if he asked them to kill her."

I left it at that, saw myself out. On the street outside, I turned back to look at his house, a semi-detached ex-council property with a small front garden. It was everything Burns wanted. A veneer of respectability, the working class man done good. Even on the inside, the place was all appearance. What you saw was exactly what he wanted you to see.

Except the lie was transparent.

Chapter 25

Rachel called, asked me to meet her.

I didn't want to go, but I had no choice.

The rain was gentle, barely noticeable. It thickened the atmosphere a little, but you only noticed it when you stood still long enough for a thin film of liquid to gather on your skin.

I came in through the east entrance, walked between the gravestones. Looked up to where the Balgay hill rolled into the graveyard. At the top of the hill, the western necropolis lurked beneath a cover of thick trees. The older graves were wild and overgrown and the world at the top of the hill seemed separate and alien compared to the uniformed regimentation of the headstones in the newer plots below.

Rachel was dressed in a heavy overcoat and carried a black umbrella. She looked up as I arrived, smiled in greeting. No emotional weight behind the expression.

I stopped where I was. Realised I would look as though I was afraid.

Maybe I was.

Rachel came to me, instead. "Last time we were here, the weather wasn't much better."

"Maybe that says something."

"Maybe." She shivered slightly. "You look ill, McNee."

"Tired, maybe."

"That's it."

"It's work."

"It's always work."

"All work and no play..."

"Makes Ja—"

I shook my head. She caught the gesture, stopped talking, But it seemed to amuse her all the same.

The moment was lost, however, when she turned to look behind her. Back at the grave where she had been standing before I arrived.

"Do you ever come here?"

I didn't know how to respond. She took that as my best answer.

"Jesus, McNee... Do you think you'll let yourself get over it? I've been up a few times. Just to come here. Talk to her, let her know how we're doing. I think about calling you, but I think you'll call when you're ready."

"What made it different this time?"

"It was her birthday. There was this gap at the table and we were all there and none of us knew what to say. And I guess I realised you were the last connection we have to her."

"Try telling your dad."

"Try talking to him."

I took a step away from her.

"You don't talk to me. You don't talk to her. No wonder you're walking around looking like someone's dropped the whole bloody world on your shoulders."

"It's not…"

"Tell me, who do you talk to?"

I couldn't think of a way to avoid the question.

Rachel didn't even give me a chance. "You and Susan were good friends. But the way she talked to you… like you didn't even know each other any more."

"I guess we drifted…"

"And there was something else, as well," she said. Her brow had furrowed gently. "Don't think I didn't notice."

My throat was dry. I knew that even if I tried to speak, I wouldn't be able to say anything. My heart pumped hard. Fight or flight, they call it. In my case: all flight.

"That was…"

"Only natural."

It took me a moment to say, "What?"

"I saw it between you, whatever this thing was. I don't know if anything happened, or if it did, but I know… I know Elaine knew you were close, the two of you. And she didn't mind because she knew that you loved her. She was secure in that."

I didn't think I gave anything away, but Rachel saw something in my face. Her own features softened for a moment. "I know why you don't want to move on, McNee. But one way or another you have to do it. You can't just isolate yourself from everyone."

She looked up at the grey skies. "You know, I'm not even going to ask that you keep in touch. If you want to, that's what you'll do. But you need to find something in your life outside of this thing that you do. Because if that's all you are, an investigator, if that's all that defines you, then it might as well have been you who died in the crash."

Chapter 26

Back at the office, in reception, I stared at the dark stain on the wooden floor. Bill's blood.

Liman and Ayer's calling card.

I tried to look away, found it impossible. The more I looked at it, the more I felt that familiar anger building up inside my chest.

I thought about their blood spilling out on some anonymous floor. Their faces twisted in agony. Hearts slowing. Breath coming in gasps. Frantic and painful and finally useless.

How good would it feel to see that? The fear in their eyes. Finally understanding how their victims felt.

I moved through to my own office. Dialled Robertson's mobile. Left a message.

With nothing else to do, I waited. The radio played for company.

"It's three-thirty in the afternoon, and here's the latest news and weather with Tay FM!"

I thought about those Cockney bastards. And a woman dying alone; in pain with no one to help her.

"Earlier this afternoon, police were called to a house in the west end of Dundee following reports of gunfire. Officers have yet to confirm that two men were found dead at the detached house on..."

I started listening. They mentioned a street. I had been there earlier in the day. Details were thin on the ground, but they repeated that there had been gunfire and that at least two men were dead.

I would have hoped the two men were Liman and Ayer, but my luck wasn't that good. And they weren't the kind to go down so easy.

I grabbed my mobile.

Susan didn't answer.

I swore and hung up.

***

The house seemed empty. A hollowed out shell. No longer the proud home I had visited that morning. If it were possible, the building seemed to be in mourning.

The police were long gone. The only remaining evidence of their presence was ragged crime scene tape and the grass out front which had been trampled while they set up a command post.

There was a light visible inside the house. It was lonely and fragile.

I walked up the garden, knocked on the front door.

The woman who answered was in her late sixties or early seventies. Her face was pale and her eyes bloodshot. Her dark grey hair was wild. The pain on her face was open and unguarded.

Burns had told me that Katrina Egg did not love her husband.

The woman before me was being eaten up by her

love for Burns. A deep, unselfish concern for the man.

I thought: what does she see in him?

"Mrs Burns, my name is McNee..."

"I'm no talking to anyone." Trying her best to sound confident and assured. Drawing herself upright. "No the newspapers."

"I'm not a journalist."

"The coppers already talked to—"

"I'm a private investigator. I knew your husband a little."

She regarded me with a deep suspicion.

"I heard about what happened on the radio."

"Then you'll appreciate when I tell you that this is not the best time—"

"I talked to him this morning. I think that... Please, I need to know what happened."

Tears gathered in her eyes. But she maintained her strength and said, "Then talk to him if you have to talk to any bastard. It's his business that did this to him. And I'm having nothing more to do with any of you shites." She stepped back and closed the door.

Gently.

But it felt like she'd slammed it.

Chapter 27

Robertson called me back. He sounded weary.

"I don't know what to do."

"They won't stop until they get what they want," I told him.

"They killed my brother."

I was on the street outside Burns's house. The single light seemed to stare at me, like a baleful eye. I tried to ignore it, turning my back to the building and looking pointedly at the far end of the street.

And I thought that Robertson was wrong. Liman and Ayer weren't responsible for Daniel's death. They hadn't been aware of what had happened to their ex-partner.

But Robertson was scared, angry and in mourning. I let the accusation slip away and arranged to meet him somewhere he considered safe.

***

On the Fife side of the Tay, there was a picnic spot on the east side of the bridge. Not much to look at, but the views across the river were beautiful and on a summer's day, families and couples stopped to admire the view and eat their lunch.

Now, with the tourist season over and the days beginning to cool, the park was empty. I didn't have to look hard to find Robertson. He sat at one of the picnic benches. Despite the bright, crisp sunlight, he seemed hidden in shadow.

I locked up the car, walked over to the bench and took a seat next to him. He didn't look at me. Kept his gaze fixed on the water and the city beyond.

"Its all ashes," he said. "Everything I worked for. Everything I had." He spoke in a flat monotone. "My wife and son are gone. My parents are dead. My brother is a suicide and now…" He turned to look at me, his normally ruddy complexion gone white and his eyes sunk back in his head; bloodshot through lack of sleep. "Christ, they came to my house. Burnt the place down. I spent the night in my car. Parked on the side of the road and dreaming of fire. And monsters. Haven't had nightmares like that since I was a bairn. But it was just a warning, wasn't it? The fire I mean. Their way of telling me that this isn't a joke to them." He looked at me and I could see the desperate panic in his eyes. "We have to give them what they want."

Asking for my help. He couldn't do this alone.

"They came to me," I said. "Told me that I was to find you. If I didn't, they'd kill me." I didn't tell him about Bill. He didn't need to know.

He said, "I didn't ask for this."

"No one does."

When I walked away from Lindsay, I had done so for reasons that had seemed transparent at the time. An unidentifiable anger had been enough, it seemed.

But I realised now that I had walked away because I knew he could help me.

When all's said and done, you have to help yourself.

They were after me as much as Robertson, these bastards. It would have been easy to place the responsibility onto his shoulders. Say that this was his problem. His brother. His family.

His problem.

Not mine.

It would have been easy.

And it would have been wrong.

"We don't have Gordon Egg's money," I told him. Deliberately using the word, "we". Unsure whether it was for his benefit or mine. "That's the problem here. If we did, we'd just hand it over, watch them walk away."

Was it really that simple? Or was I just giving him reassurances?

Whatever, I can't say that the platitudes took much of the burden from his shoulders.

"Aye," he said. "Although... I've no been exactly honest with you. And maybe I should..." He ran his hands across his bald head, as though trying to smooth down the hair he once had. "Jesus... I know where it is. The money." He turned away again, looked at the water. His hands clasped together in front of his expansive stomach, his fingers intertwining like fleshy worms. "I didn't tell you the truth. About Daniel. When I said I hadn't seen him until I found his body, that wasn't true. He came to see me earlier that night. I didn't realise it then, but I think he was trying to say goodbye. And I should have said something, but..."

Robertson's gaze remained fixed on the river,

despite the blinding sunlight that bounced back off the silver of the water.

He took a deep breath. As he told me about the night his brother came back into his life, appearing on the doorstep like an apparition from the past, crows cried out as they circled in the sky above. Their song sounded like mocking laughter.

Chapter 28

Robertson told me the story slowly. Stumbling over words. Reluctant to let the truth out.

He said that he'd come to me, not out of idle curiosity, but out of fear. Knowing his brother was into something bad and wanting someone who could give him more information. Help him understand not only who his brother had been but why he had to take his own life.

Robertson had held back before. Not wanting to admit the truth because it scared him. Because he was afraid that somehow, just by seeing his brother for those last moments, he was responsible.

That's what he said.

On the afternoon his brother came home, James Robertson had been in his front room, drinking a large Glenfiddich. He'd attended a hunt earlier in the day, tramping through undergrowth in the countryside surrounding Perth. His companions a mix of lawyers and landowners.

The whisky was opened as soon as he arrived back home. He drank alone in a house that had never felt so empty in all the fifty-seven years of his life.

When the knock came, it toppled Robertson from his chair. He'd been slipping into sleep and the sudden noise woke him. He steadied himself and grabbed the glass from where it lay on the floor. He walked through the kitchen and out to the front door.

"To see him standing there," Robertson told me, "even after all these years, and looking so different from me, it was a shock. Like looking into one of those funny mirrors you get at the Lammas Market. Seeing yourself, only something's not quite right. I didn't know what to say. And I don't know that he did either. We just stood there. Like bloody lemons."

Daniel was the one who finally broke the stand-off, pushing past his brother and into the house with a brusqueness that verged on violence. Robertson followed the other man into the living room. But he almost turned and ran when he saw Daniel's coat-tails lift, revealing a momentary glimpse of a hunting knife tucked in his belt.

Daniel didn't bother with any of the reunion talk. He placed the briefcase he was carrying onto the coffee table and opened it.

The contents of the case made Robertson think he was having a drunk dream. Bundles of money sat snugly bunched together. There was more cash in the case than he would ever have hoped to see in his lifetime.

Robertson's heart hammered against his rib cage so hard he thought it would burst. The sweat poured off him and soaked into his shirt. He flopped into a chair and sat there, staring at his brother and the briefcase.

"I want you to have it," Daniel said. His Scots

accent had been corrupted by his years in London. "The money. All of it."

"And if I don't?"

Daniel shrugged. No big deal. As though, in his world, people got offered cases of cash in their front rooms every day. "Then get rid of it."

It was that matter-of-fact dismissal that hit Robertson hard. There had been so much he wanted to say, so many things he could have asked. They could have talked about their father, about the years growing up together that they had lost. They could have drunk a glass of whisky in their mother's memory.

But they did none of that.

Because Robertson found himself frightened by the money and the knife and what kind of man his brother must have become to enter his house with these things.

The way Robertson told the story, Daniel had left with barely another word. Gone like a ghost. Robertson would have been tempted to put the whole thing down to some kind of drunken hallucination, if not for the evidence left behind.

The money.

The case.

***

Robertson looked close to tears. He took off his bunnet and scrunched it up in his hands. Refusing to look me in the eye, he said, "I knew that the money was tainted when I saw it. Just knew. Right here." He thumped his chest. His eyes were tearing up. He blinked a few times. "He was like those villains you see on the TV, the ones who'd kill you as soon as look at you. And I thought... if this is how he turned out...The apple doesn't fall far from the tree, right? We shared something, Daniel and me. I just couldn't believe that he'd turn out..."

His fists clenched tight. His knuckles went white with the strain.

"I lied to you," he said. "The police, too. Do you know how that felt? When I've never done anything like that in my life? No until he showed up on my doorstep. Aye, but what else could I do? I should have given them the money, everything. When they asked... If I'd done that..." He laughed. It was bitter and forced; anything to stop those tears flowing.

I wanted to ask why he didn't. But I didn't.

I felt nauseous, hoped it didn't show in my expression. I waited a few seconds and said, "Your brother wasn't a bad apple. But landing where he did, the rot set in. I don't think it was all his fault. Maybe he could have chosen to walk away from all the bad shit that finally killed him, I don't know. Sometimes we don't have a choice in these things. But I think all that he wanted was a life that was worth more than the farm could ever be. He wanted to be something else. And he got that dream. But at a price."

"Aye," said Robertson. "Maybe, when he was hanging from that tree, feeling the rope cut into his neck, he finally understood that." He had an odd look to his face: a cold expression that dried up the moistness of his eyes. His features set themselves in a way that made me think of his brother's mugshot: that same pride and intensity.

I tried not to shiver.

"Sure," I said, agreeing more out of habit than anything else. "But I want you to understand something. I don't care whether you lied to protect your brother's name or whether there's something else going on here. You've landed us both in the shit. I get it, why you didn't go back to the police when I asked you to the first time. Still afraid they'd see through your lie. They'd question your motives. They wouldn't believe anything as simple as a fraternal bond. I can't think of anyone who would be comfortable with the police sniffing around their life looking for something that wasn't there. Because we're all guilty." I let it hang too long. Added, lamely, "Of something."

He looked at me for a moment and then said, "So tell me, McNee, why haven't you gone to the police? You could have gone at any time. Washed your hands of me and my brother and this whole mess."

"What happened to the money?" I asked, avoiding his question.

"I kept it. Thought maybe he'd come back." Whether that was delusion or a lie, I wasn't sure.

"But he never did. Were you planning on using it?" I asked.

"I hadn't thought about... Christ, what a question to ask." He bit his bottom lip and lowered his eyes so that he didn't have to look at me.

I felt a chill in the air. No wind, no clear sign of the temperature dropping, but it was there nonetheless. And I knew, watching his face, that Robertson felt it, too.

Chapter 29

"We don't have a choice, do we?" Robertson said. "We have to give them what they want."

I kept my gaze fixed on the placid surface of the Tay and the splintered sunlight that reflected off the water. Jesus, what was I doing?

"If we give them the money, they'll leave us alone." A hint of desperation in his voice.

I turned to face him. "Do you really believe that?"

"What else can we do?"

I struggled to find a response. Thinking about Rachel telling me how selfish I was.

Susan, in my office, telling me I was stubborn and foolish not to trust Lindsay.

Andy turning his back on me when I tried to talk to him about Bill.

Elaine's father, his voice on the other end of the phone, tight and controlled as he told me I was a murderer and he would see me in jail if it killed him too.

And rage.

Rage that had been waiting so long to find a release.

"We can still go to the police," I said. "We don't have to do this."

"If you believe that, then why haven't you gone to them?"

I'd avoided his question once. I wanted to tell him that I had gone to the police. But the truth was that my conversation with Lindsay had been a smoke-screen; a way of making myself feel as though I had at least tried to do the right thing.

"We give these thugs their money," I said. "We tell them to leave. And that's the end to it. They have nothing to fear from us."

"Aye," said Robertson. "After all, who are we to them?"

But I saw it in his face. He knew I was lying. Even if he had believed me, I knew the shame that gathered like rocks in my stomach would still have weighed me down as I realised that this could only end badly.

***

Driving back across the bridge, I was still thinking about Robertson's question: "If you believe that, then why haven't you gone to them?"

Lindsay had said I was pissing on someone else's territory, that I did this kind of thing because I was a selfish prick. Could he have a point? Part of me was beginning to question my own motives, as though I couldn't even trust myself any more.

Not that it mattered. Over the last few days, I'd regressed to where I'd been after the accident: retreating inwards. Seeking solace with grim reflections on the violence and suffering that I had encountered. The difference was that now I could definitively deal with these feelings. I had someone to blame.

Real.

Tangible.

I could hurt them.

Again, I imagined the life fading from their eyes. Their blood on the ground.

Knowing that no one would regret their deaths. Not after everything they had done.

As I drove across the bridge, the heat of the late afternoon sun warmed my skin. I thought about the fire that had burned Robertson's house to the ground. The smoke that had choked up the sky.

When I was a copper, I arrested a fifteen year old boy who liked to set fire to things. He'd started out small, with insects, but quickly graduated onto abandoned buildings. I caught him trying to burn an abandoned mill on Guthrie Street. He had later responded well in the interview, but what I remembered most was when he said, "I love fire. Flames. They get me hard."

"Why?"

"Release, isn't it? Fire fucking purifies everything. Burns what you don't need."

And I realised that what I was doing was starting a little fire of my own. Waiting for purification and for the past to crumble away into ashes.

Chapter 30

"Can't say I thought much of your message."

Susan stood in the door. In full uniform. Her expression stern.

If I was a crook, I wouldn't have stood a chance.

"I didn't really intend to leave one."

She nodded, walked in. Stopped when she saw the faded bloodstain on the floor.

"How is he? Your friend."

"He's fine. I think."

"You think?"

"I haven't been to see him. I called, but..."

"He can't blame you."

"His boyfriend can."

She considered that for a moment. "My mother would have said you'd make a fine martyr."

I didn't ask what Susan would say.

Tearing her gaze away from the floor, she said, "The DI said you came to see him the other day."

"That was a mistake. I thought I had something to say and... I didn't."

"Maybe. He asked me if I could have a word with

you. Said he thought I might be able to convince you to see sense."

"Aye?"

"Right enough, seeing as he thinks we're friends."

"Are we?"

She walked past the desk, dropped into the recliner. "I'm not a little girl, Steed. I'm not going to pretend I wasn't hurt by what happened but... you were in mourning and I was... in my own place. We needed each other."

"That has nothing to do with it."

"It has everything to do with it. It's the way you are. Someone reaches out and you pull away. Always amazed me how she ever managed to make you love her in the first place."

My stomach tightened. "Don't bloody do this."

"I'm sorry, Steed. But you can't go around treating everyone like the enemy. Some of us are your friends. Hell, even a prick like Lindsay, he isn't out to get you. He's not the bad guy."

"Bastard's turned you around."

"Lindsay's a good copper. Maybe it doesn't make him a great human being, but it doesn't make him an evil bastard, either." Her face softened. "Maybe I said some things before... in the heat of the moment. You bring that out in people."

"Yeah?" I thought of Elaine's father. The heat of the moment lasting almost a year.

"Yeah," she said. "I always liked you, Steed, you know that? Always thought your heart was in the right place."

Susan wasn't the type of person to backtrack. She'd always been straightforward, meaning every word she said.

"Four people have died," Susan said. "Because of

something you know or something your client, the farmer, knows." And there she was: Constable Susan, again. Her humanity gone, hidden behind the armour that every copper needs to wear on the job.

"Four people?"

"Daniel Robertson. Katrina Egg. And the two men who died this afternoon. That's why you called me, right?" A crack appeared in her armour, but only for a moment. "They were no accounts, really. Local hard men. Shot to death in Burns's front hall. Burns himself... someone gave him a real good kicking. He's stable, but refusing to talk. No surprise there. He says he can't think of a reason why he was attacked. He didn't know his assailants. A mugging. His words, not ours." I must have let something slip, because she kept going. "And you know something, right, Steed? Or at least you have your suspicions."

I shook my head.

But I had more than just suspicions.

"This is a police matter, now. You can keep your client confidentiality and all that other nonsense as close to your chest as you want. If you keep pushing us away, more people are going to get hurt."

I clenched my jaw, pushed my teeth together so tight it began to hurt, the pain shooting up the side of my face and pounding into my head.

"So maybe you want to think about it," she said.

I stood, quiet for a moment, unsure how to respond. And then: "If you were anyone else, I'd have told you go fuck yourself."

She stepped back, holding her breath. I thought maybe she was about to explode, but instead she merely let out a little sigh. "I thought I knew you a little better, Steed," she said, before turning to walk out of the office.

I waited a moment, went out on the stairwell. Found her card lying at the top of the stairs. Maybe she expected me to call her when I calmed down. I picked up the card, screwed it up in my fist and let it drop back to the floor.

When I went back into the office, I upended Bill's desk.

And then tried to work out if I felt any better.

Chapter 31

I was back at the hospital early that evening.

Not to see Bill. I had other concerns.

A heavy-set man stood outside the private room, large arms folded across his expansive chest. The doctors and nurses passing the door kept their distance.

I made to walk through like the big man wasn't even there.

He grabbed me by the shoulder. Tight. Even underneath the baggy shellsuit he was wearing, it was clear that his bulk was all muscle. He brought his face close to mine. Assaulted me with stale breath.

"Can I ask your business?" Polite but threatening.

"My name's McNee," I said. "He knows who I am."

"What do you want with Mr Burns?" Enunciating each word as if I hadn't heard him the first time.

"It's private."

He looked at me suspiciously and then said, "Hold on," motioning for me to wait. He opened the door and walked inside.

A doctor walked past, eyed me suspiciously. "I didn't realise you employed private security," I said. He kept walking, his head down.

I could have listened, but I didn't think there'd be anything worth hearing. Besides, if the walking meat slab came out and found me eavesdropping, I doubted he'd wait to hear my excuses. Probably make sure I got my own private room.

When he came out, he said, "In you go."

I moved past him. Inside the room, there was a single window on the far wall and a toilet area through a second door. But Burns wasn't getting up to go anywhere.

When I saw him that morning he had been an old man who still buzzed with the anger of his youth. Unafraid, unbowed, and unbroken.

Now, his reputation, everything he had worked so hard to maintain, had been stripped from him. I looked at him wrapped in white hospital sheets, his face lined and his skin pale where it wasn't blotted dark with bruises. A corpse that didn't realise it was supposed to be dead.

"Take a seat." His voice was soft, lacking the edge I'd noted during our last conversation.

I sat down, made sure the chair stayed a good distance from the bed.

"Your limp's looking better, son."

I hadn't even thought about it. Seven months ago when I'd come to the hospital for my last session, the psychiatrist had said, "You know there's nothing wrong with your leg." I'd called him on talking crap. "I've seen your medical records. Okay, you were hurt in the accident, but you should be on the mend. I have to wonder whether it's something else."

It wasn't supposed to be our last session, but that's

168

when I told him where he could stick his analysis.

"You owe me," Burns said when I failed to acknowledge his observation.

"I don't owe you anything," I said. "What's changed for me? What's changed for my client?"

"I put my fucking life on the line for you and your client, son," he said and if his voice had been capable of it, he would have shouted. However, the words came out weak and hushed. "Look at what it got me."

"They didn't kill you."

"No bastard's going to kill me."

I shook my head. "They meant to leave you alive."

"A mistake."

"No, I don't think it was. They're saying that you're nothing. They want you to know that they don't care if you live. Because you can't touch them."

"That's a mistake, too. These pricks, they can't help making them."

"You and your kind don't lash out at each other for no good reason. At least not the old school fellas. You've got a code of honour, even vicious bastards like Egg. So this was personal."

He couldn't look me in the eye.

"Five years ago, you would have quietly had those two bastards disappear the minute that woman turned up dead. It was an affront to you. On your turf, no less. Gordon Egg wouldn't have batted an eyelid if you'd taught them a lesson. You and Egg are such close friends that his men should accord you a certain amount of respect on your home turf. Unless all of that's changed and you just didn't bother making it public knowledge. Because God knows how much damage that could do to your reputation elsewhere."

I scratched the chair forward across the floor, getting in close. Adrenaline rushed through me. My face was hot and it was an effort to speak as my jaw clenched. I felt like finishing the job that Egg's thugs had started.

The words came out slow and measured. "You knew all of that when I came to see you. You knew you were fucked, that you couldn't help me even if you wanted to. But I guess it was some misplaced pride made you pretend you could still do anything you wanted. You're getting sloppy in your old age. Funny, isn't it? Egg's on top and he's making sure he kicks you all the way down to the bottom. Maybe already grooming some smart young thing to take your place? Who's the next big player up here, eh? Or do you want me to ask around? Since I guess you're no longer in the loop."

His breathing changed. Slower, now. Harder. Forcing himself to keep calm. The veins stood out in his neck. "Do you know about the two dead lads?" he asked.

"It was on the news. A couple of thugs."

"Aye, you fucking prick. Call them that if you like, but they were some mother's sons. Good lads."

Did he ever think, I wondered, about the people he'd killed? Realise that they, too, were some mother's sons?

I doubted that it ever crossed his mind.

"I'm going to be around for a long time yet, son," he said. "And that fucking turncoat cunt, he'll be fucking sorry his lads didn't kill me."

I stood up. "I know them."

He looked at me with dead eyes.

"I know their names," I said. "Tell me about them."

170

"Are you going to go crying to the police with their names, tell the coppers about the bad boys who threatened you?"

I shook my head. "I'm going to ask them to leave. No middle men. No police."

"Ask them to leave?" he said, his tone carefully neutral. "Just like that?"

I nodded. "Just like that," I said.

Burns grinned. "Did he jump or was he pushed?" he said, talking to himself, mulling over the question.

And he smiled. It was not a comforting expression. Showing something of the man who had greeted me in his kitchen the day before. Maybe he wasn't so beaten as I'd allowed myself to believe. "I think I'm beginning to know the answer, son."

Chapter 32

He told me what he could.

"First time I heard of these lads was maybe ten years ago. When Gordon Egg noticed their... unique talents."

They'd been with the big man's firm maybe five years before that, although they were little more than foot soldiers and it was likely Egg hadn't even been aware of them until they started working for him in Brixton.

"Christ, they earned their stars there. Started bringing in three or four times the revenue the big man expected." Talking about Egg's firm like it was a rival business. "He started asking around, found out who brought them in. That's where things started going wrong, because their contact was your dead man. Daniel Robertson."

I already knew Daniel had been close to Egg. It was one hell of a reference for two small-time hard men.

They way Burns told it, Egg began handing out choice jobs to the lads and, impressed with their ability to dish out pain, started pulling them up the ladder. "Nobody grumbled. Nobody had the fucking balls to grumble."

By the tail end of the nineties, Daniel Robertson, Mathew Ayer and Richard Liman were working together as equals. They had become the public face of the firm as Egg drifted into the background, determined to make his new found respectability seem legit.

"He knew soon enough he'd made a mistake," Burns told me.

The mistake was putting Ayer and Liman on a level with the man who had brought them into the organisation. Creating a situation that was unstable at best. As the years passed, the unholy trinity that Egg had created began to show cracks. Rumours of violent confrontations between all three men began to spread through the firm.

And through it all, Egg did nothing.

"After all, what the fuck could he do? Admit he made a mistake? Jesus Christ, you don't do that. Not in our life, eh? So he did what he could, and tried to make things right between the lads."

Except it was a case of two against one. Liman and Ayer had come into the firm together, worked at their best together. They were inseparable. "A fucking married couple. Except instead of saying they love each other, they kneecap poor bastards who can't keep up their debts."

In the last two years, the three men had rarely worked together. The only thing that kept them from killing each other, it seemed, was Egg himself. "The old bastard has this going for him: he knows how to keep a man under control. Jesus, in another world, he'd be running the fucking country."

And then Liman and Ayer got the advantage, discovered that Daniel had been having an affair with Egg's wife.

Burns had already told me about Katrina Egg's infidelities.

What made this affair so different?

The fact that Daniel had been set up as Egg's golden child? The dual betrayal too much for the old bastard to handle?

Or he'd finally had enough?

"Each time she'd come running back to her man. Apologetic, teary-eyed. And he'd forgive her. The thing was, this time she wasn't going to come back. She was leaving with Daniel. That was the plan. But of course, with Liman and Ayer getting wind of it... everything got fucked up. Daniel got out, but she didn't."

Except Daniel didn't leave empty handed. If he and Kat were going to make a new life, they'd need cash, a way of keeping themselves afloat. Two days prior to his arrival in Dundee, Daniel ripped off a small fortune from the old man's personal stash.

"After that, no turning back, eh? Just a pity those two fucks dropped him in it. Egg confronted his wife, Daniel got scared and disappeared with the money."

"And then he killed himself?"

Burns didn't seem to worry about the contradiction between Daniel's apparent desire to escape the life and his suicide shortly afterwards. "Looks that way, aye."

Something didn't sit right, but Burns either didn't give a shit or had just never considered the question.

Burns had never made the connection to Daniel Robertson's suicide. He read something in the paper about a farmer's estranged brother hanging himself

174

in the woods and never gave it a second thought. The police had made sure any mention of Daniel's life in London stayed out of the papers.

It was only when Gordon Egg called him to ask a favour that Burns realised what was going on.

My phone call to the club had got Katrina Egg's attention. She'd been there that day, under the watchful eye of Egg's boys. She'd overheard my first phone call to the club, then called me back to try and see if I could tell her anything about Daniel. She didn't know where he'd gone by then. Their plan had been fucked, and all she knew was that her lover was running scared from her husband.

The next day she'd slipped out from under the eyes of her minders and made for the North. Egg, no fool, worked out where she was heading, piecing together the information in the same way as his wife had done. He knew there were only two people he could trust to sort out this mess: the men who had told him about his wife's affair in the first place.

"He called me, said he was sending those two bastards up here. Told me why. It was only after they arrived that I realised what had happened, who that cunt in the forest was."

But Liman and Ayer weren't here for Daniel Robertson. They wanted Katrina Egg. And they knew that she could lead them to the money as well.

Burns gave them everything they needed. "And they fucked me over."

Leaving the body in the flat Burns had "loaned them".

It wasn't her death that concerned him. Burns didn't care about that. As far as he was concerned, it didn't matter why they killed her, either. Whether they were acting under Egg's orders or whether things got out of control.

All that mattered to Burns was that they'd left a trail of evidence that led right to his door.

"You want to know something about those two bastards?" said Burns. "I'll tell you all you need to know, son. They're stone cold psychopaths. They don't think like you and me. If they want you dead, then you're dead. They won't fucking blink. My advice for you and your... client... is to get out of the town. Just fucking walk. You should know, son, the police can do fuck all to help you."

"Tell me what happened this afternoon," I said.

"What more do you need to know?"

"I need to know why Egg told his men to hurt you. Because if they've done this to you, then..."

Burns grinned, lips parting to reveal yellow wolf-like teeth. "They really fucking got to you."

"Just tell me."

Chapter 33

When Burns talked about the events of that afternoon, I saw something in his face. His jaw seemed tight and his eyes focused on mine, trying to hold me, make me understand the importance of what he was telling me.

He didn't care about the death of Katrina Egg.

But he cared about his own mortality.

After I left his house, he'd thought about what I'd said. Burns could be described as an arrogant man, but his ego wasn't big enough to make him stupid. He could see that some of what I had said made sense.

If he allowed the situation to go unchecked, he might as well let these two Cockney Rotweiller's fuck him in his own backyard.

So he called two lads who did door work at one of his pubs. Took them to see Liman and Ayer.

Taught the two Cockney bastards a lesson. Taught them respect.

Afterwards, he had a quiet pint with the two lads who had provided the muscle. "Hardly conversationalists, aye, but good boys. Know their place, eh?"

Despite his earlier protestations that these two were some mother's sons, he never once referred to them by name.

Burns tried to call Egg several times. Every time the phone rang out. He left messages. He waited.

He got nothing.

When he arrived home that afternoon, he asked the two lads to wait with him.

"I wasn't scared. But if those two Cockney cunts came looking for revenge, I wasn't facing them alone. I'm no exactly a young man any more, aye?"

Everything he told me was qualified; backed up by some excuse for behaviour he saw as weak or cowardly.

He couldn't tell me outright that he had been scared.

Burns had been in the kitchen, sitting at the breakfast bar and reading that day's *Tele*. Katrina Egg's murder dominated the news, but she had not yet been named. For "legal" reasons, according to the report. He allowed himself a smile at that.

When he heard a knock at the door, he sent one of the two lads to answer. Expecting some journalist prick or maybe the police back again to harass him.

There were raised voices and a gunshot.

Burns headed for the back door. Like the man said, he wasn't stupid.

More voices. A second gunshot.

Burns's hand was on the door handle. He was ready to run out into the back yard.

A voice said, "Don't even fucking think about it."

Burns knew that it was over. And he'd be fucked if he was going to die with a bullet in his back.

He turned, slowly, with his hands raised.

Let the bastards look into his eyes before they killed him.

Liman stood in the doorway, holding a shotgun. The psychotic, bald prick was smiling.

"Take a picture," said Burns. "It'll last longer."

Another gunshot from the hallway.

Then Ayer came through, dragging one of Burns's bodyguards. He had the younger man by the hair, his free hand holding the handgun that was clearly responsible for the blood seeping out of the lad's belly.

"If you're going to shoot me," Burns said, "just fucking do it."

Burns had stepped forward, his arms open wide. These two men were cowards, he knew. He believed they wouldn't shoot him if he invited them to. Their pride wouldn't allow it.

They didn't shoot.

Ayer let go of the man with the bleeding stomach. The lad collapsed on the floor.

Burns looked Ayer in the eyes. "Fucking do it, then. Kill me."

Ayer slammed the butt of the handgun into Burns's face.

The old gangster was on his knees before he knew what was happening. Someone kicked him in the chest and he was on his back. He tasted blood thick in the back of his throat. His eyes watered and the whole world turned to a blur.

He was nearly deafened by a final gunshot.

He knew the lad they'd dragged in from the hallway was dead.

And he thought, as he felt the two Cockney hard men kicking him about the head and ribs, that he would be dead soon, as well.

He lost all sense of place, only aware of the pain as their boots smashed into his body.

And when he thought it was nearly over, that his body was ready to simply give up and die, he heard a voice say, "Gordon Egg says fuck you, you cunt."

***

When he was finished, Burns looked at me. "You wanted to know, son." Mouth set. Gaze steady.

"Do you still think you can just give these pricks what they want and they'll walk away?"

I didn't even try to answer. Instead, I asked, "Why didn't they kill you?"

His lips parted. Might have been a smile if he hadn't killed it so quick.

"I have a son. He's not like me. He's an accountant, aye? Moved away from the old man, tried to pretend he was someone else. Christ, I never knew where he got that from... But a prick like you... I see something in your eyes that reminds me of who I was when I was a young man."

"You should cut back on the morphine," I said. "You're beginning to hallucinate."

"Did you jump or were you pushed? I told you I thought I could see the answer. You don't want to give these cunts what they were after. Or turn them in to the police. No, I see what you want. You want to fuck them up. Show them who the real hard man is. And you can dress it up however you like, because you like to pretend you're the hero. Makes you feel better, right? But in the end, it comes down to one simple thing: you're spoiling for a fight."

I didn't tell him he was wrong.

Instead, I stood up and walked out of the room. I had everything I needed.

He didn't throw out a parting shot. And that worried me more than anything he could have said.

Chapter 34

Bill's bed was in a bay of six, positioned at the far end, close to the large window that would allow the ward to be flooded with light during the day.

He was upright, with his eyes closed and a battered paperback discarded on his lap.

There was a strange air of peace surrounding him. Despite the bruises and the discolouration of his face, he might have been asleep.

Asleep and hooked up to an IV.

A nurse stood beside me, her brow furrowed. "Visiting hours ended at eight."

"I'm sorry," I said. "I wasn't thinking. I just…"

"Unless you have business here, I'll have to ask you to leave."

"How's he doing, the man in the end bed?"

"Are you a relative?"

"A friend."

"He's doing well. Recovering."

"Yeah, he looks good."

The nurse didn't say anything. She bit her bottom

lip and kept her gaze fixed on Bill.

"If you want, I can take a message. Let him know you were here."

"No. Not yet."

As I turned to leave, she placed a hand on my forearm, but the touch was fleeting and I slipped away fast.

***

Back at my flat, I grabbed a nap on the sofa. The alarm on my mobile set to wake me up in an hour.

I was exhausted, physically and mentally. In need of a recharge.

And then someone started hammering the front door.

Blearily, I answered, saw Burns's polite gorilla from the hospital. His expression might have been carved in granite. His deep set eyes stared straight over my head. We stood there for a long time before he held out a paper bag and said, "A present."

"A present?"

"Just take it."

Relenting, finally, I took it from him. Felt a dead weight in there.

"I wasn't here," said the gorilla. "And you never had a wee chat with the boss. Aye?" He walked away before I had a chance to reply. I waited until I heard the downstairs door slam shut before slipping back inside my flat.

I hobbled through to the kitchen, thinking I must have been lying the wrong way. Pins and needles fired up and down my leg.

I put the bag on the worktop. Hesitated for a moment before I reached inside and pulled out a handgun; semi-automatic. I'd never handled one, but you don't spend a few years on the force without picking up a little firearms knowledge.

I laid it down on the worktop, reached inside the bag once more. Found a handwritten note.

McNee
We have a common purpose, you and me. You would deny it but we're closer than you'd like to admit. We both have that fire within us. I saw it in your eyes.

Liman and Ayer are no joke. Someone should have dealt with them long before now. They're not scared of you or the police. They're not scared of anyone. There's one language they understand and you have to convince them that you speak it well, before they kill you. This wee gift should help.

No need to say thank you.

Unsigned. Not that it needed a signature.

I looked at the gun again. Turned it over. Checked the safety. Hit the release. Ejected the cartridge.

Not even thinking about getting rid of the damn thing.

I examined the stacked bullets. Wondered how something so small could be so deadly. They looked like nothing important. Innocent pieces of metal.

I placed the cartridge down on the worktop next to the gun. Hunted around until I found an old pair of leather gloves. Wiped down the gun, taking my time. No fingerprints.

My mobile rang.

On the other end of the line, Robertson said, "I've got the money. They called. We're ready to go."

"Where?"

"Balgay Cemetery. Well, the Necropolis."

I shivered, thought of those ancient graves on top of the hill, their ragged formation rolling and morphing into the regimentation of Balgay Cemetery.

"Midnight," he said. "At the Hird Bridge."

In my mind, I saw rows of graves and thought about Elaine's body beneath the ground. Seeing her not as a corpse but the way she used to look when she was sleeping next to me.

I felt like I was in there with her, my chest tightening and my breathing becoming shallow.

Heard the panicked rhythm of her heartbeat beside me.

I told Robertson I'd be there and hung up the phone.

Went through to the kitchen. Staggering a little, my balance shot.

I told myself this was nothing more than a bad dream.

And it worked. For a moment.

I grabbed a mug from the kitchen cupboard. The cold of the china shocked me, and my hand spasmed. The mug slipped from my fingers, bounced off the kitchen worktop and smashed on the floor.

Chapter 35

One particular memory. The one I wish I could wipe forever:

I looked to my right, saw Elaine in the driver's seat.

It's the little details that stick in your mind.

Her hair.

The way it looked in the darkness of the car, illuminated by the backwash of the headlights and the dashboard lights.

Her eyes.

Focused on the road ahead and with a harshness to them that made me feel uncomfortable, reminding me of what we had said to each other only minutes earlier.

My gaze shifted, and I saw her father reflected in the rear view mirror. His face was set in a grim expression. His eyes locked onto mine.

We drove along winding country roads. On either side, trees lined up like soldiers. Their upper branches bent forwards to create a canopy that blotted out the night sky.

Martin Barrow said, "Maybe now isn't the time to

discuss this." His voice rumbled, made me shiver.

Elaine said, "You're right, Dad, it isn't the time." Her tone sharp. Sharper than when she talked to me? I doubted it.

Stupid little arguments.

The kind you look back on, realise how unimportant they were. Or worse, how you were the one in the wrong.

I looked out of the passenger window, watched her reflection. Her head was held high, and her gaze had become fixed on the road ahead. Like me, she didn't want to have the conversation again. What could we say that hadn't already been said?

Except her dad didn't know about the conversation we'd had on Elaine's birthday three nights earlier. The conversation that had ended badly, neither of us able to properly apologise until the sun came up the next morning.

This evening, we'd been to see a friend of the family. Her family, of course. The friend now a mother, with a tiny baby girl.

We'd talked about it before: children, family, stability.

Sometimes shouting more than actually talking.

I said, every time, that we should wait. Think things over.

Like I said, you look back, you realise you were in the wrong.

The arguments covered up the fact that the conversations scared me. That I had doubts and insecurities I couldn't admit to her. I would realise that in time.

From the back seat, Elaine's father said, "You've no right to speak to her like that."

I said, "I just mean that we're not ready. If

something were to happen, I..."

Elaine turned her head. Taking her eyes off the road, her mind focused not on the car but on me and my selfish fucking stupidity.

"How long do you want to wait? Another five years? Ten? Longer?"

That was all it took. A momentary distraction. A few seconds of anger.

One argument over nothing and then —

Katrina Egg's dead eyes staring at me, accusingly.

Andy turning away from me in the hospital.

Bill bleeding out on the floor of the office.

— a sudden, intense glare sliced through my vision. The bastard driving full beam. I saw Elaine's pupils contract as the headlights from the other car illuminated her face with its white light.

The grey Peugeot was out of control. Over on our side of the road. Elaine twisted the wheel so we moved to the other lane.

My hand reached out to touch Elaine.

An apology?

I don't know if I could say for sure.

I heard what sounded like thunder, felt the world lurch.

I closed my eyes. Felt gravity try to tear my body through the floor of the car.

A million fists pounded me.

A high pitched noise assaulted my ears as metal crunched and creased.

And then silence.

Stillness.

At some point I had crawled from the car, but I couldn't remember how it happened. Found myself on my hands and knees in the grass that swayed back and forth in the night-time breeze. I stared back at the road, through the remains of the broken dyke. Elaine's car had rolled down the incline and now it was behind me. Turned over on its roof, the wheels still spinning. The horn screamed, shattering the still of the country night.

I looked for any sign of the other car.

Saw nothing.

As though it had never been there.

I tried to get to my feet, found my left leg supported no weight and collapsed beneath me. There was no pain.

I pulled myself along the ground towards the overturned car, gripping handfuls of earth and grass and feeling the dead weight of my legs try to hold me back.

I couldn't see Elaine. Her father lay halfway out of the car, the back door opened as though he had made an attempt to exit the vehicle before finally giving up and passing out.

But where was Elaine?

I knew the answer. But tried not to think about it as I crawled to find her body among the screaming mass of twisted metal that lay overturned among the untamed grass.

Chapter 36

I steadied myself against the kitchen worktop. Looked at the shattered mug on the floor. Felt sick.

Finally, I cleared up the mess, poured myself tap water. My hands trembling as I held a glass beneath the tap.

I drank the water slowly.

Remembered Rachel asking me why I never went to Elaine's grave. The lie I had told myself was that by performing my vigil at the scene of the accident that brought me somehow closer to her.

But here was the truth: I was afraid to go to her grave because that would make her death absolute. So concrete that it could never be taken back. It would remind me of my own responsibility. Something that was brought home to me when I saw the look in her father's eyes as he watched his youngest daughter's casket lowered gently into the earth.

***

I sat in the living room. In the dark.

I looked at my watch, illuminated by the moonlight sneaking through the window. Eleven o'clock. An hour before I had to meet Robertson at the top of the Balgay hill, across the other side of the iron bridge that would take us to the Western Necropolis.

I threw on a pair of dark jeans, a black polo neck and a long, winter coat that sat heavy on my shoulders.

In the kitchen, I pulled on my leather gloves and picked up the gun. Checked the safety. Slipped it into my coat pocket where it bumped gently against my thigh.

In the car, I drove to the steady, portentous rhythms of Nick Cave and the Bad Seeds singing of a town called Tupelo.

I parked on Scott Street. Outside, the night air was sharp.

Ahead of me, at the end of the street, was the Balgay hill. Thick trees and bushes concealed another world there. One hidden from the urbanity that surrounded the hill.

I walked slowly into Balgay park, followed the roughly marked path up the side of the hill. The sound of my heartbeat echoed through the night. The city traffic faded, becoming background noise until finally it didn't exist at all. At the peak of the hill, the Hird Bridge crossed to where the Western Necropolis sat shrouded under tall trees.

I still hadn't managed to shake the pins and needles.

Maybe I should have unpacked the crutches.

The Hird Bridge passed over an old path that led from Dunkeld Place past the Necropolis and into Balgay park. A local legend claimed that a phantom coach ran under the bridge on nights when the moon was full. See the coach and you'd die shortly afterwards.

A legend. But late at night even a legend can seem real. Shadows have a nasty way of making ghosts seem plausible.

I strained hard to hear the noises of the night. At the first hint of hooves, my eyes would be closed.

Although I tried not to look down between the gaps in the iron bridge, I found my eyes drawn there. It took a tremendous amount of willpower to force my gaze up. The full moon peeked out from behind thick, dark clouds. Normally impassive, the ancient symbol of madness seemed somehow apprehensive.

A twig snapped somewhere behind me. I turned and saw Robertson. Carrying a smart, grey briefcase. It seemed anachronistic in his grasp. Too business-like, as though he'd mugged a still-stuck-in-the-eighties yuppie. His clothes didn't help. A thick, padded farmer's jacket and his bunnet balanced precariously on his head.

"I need this to be over," he said, wiping his free hand across his face to remove sweat. His breathing was loud and jittery. Made me think of Burns in the hospital, hyperventilating.

The weather had been close for much of the day. Threatening thunder. Now, in the distance, a low and distant rumble signalled a storm sloping towards the city.

I looked at my watch. Two minutes to midnight. We walked across the bridge in silence. The stone beneath my feet sang out when my boots slammed down.

I heard a rhythmic patter that made me think of the phantom coach. After a moment, I realised the noise was nothing more than the rush of blood through my veins and the rapid rhythm of my own heart.

Robertson had stopped, too, several steps behind me. He started again, his breathing, ragged and out of control and his feet landing heavily with each step. I couldn't help but think of him breaking through the aged metal and plummeting to the path below.

Across the other side we walked through the arch that led into the Necropolis. I checked my watch. One minute to midnight.

We waited in the shadow of a family tomb that stood to the left of the arch; proud and lonely, separated from the rest of the Necropolis. Whether by accident or design, I was unsure.

I looked for some sign of the family, saw no telltale inscription on the visible surface of the structure. Perhaps their names were hidden by the dark.

My heart thumped hard, enough that it resonated across my ribs. I thought about turning back, walking away. I had come here for my own selfish ends, to lay to rest ghosts which only existed in my own mind. So much for the professional detachment I claimed to hold so dear.

Looking at my companion, I realised I still didn't understand why he was here, or what he hoped to gain by all of this. As he stood there beside the tomb of some unnamed family, I found he was hidden in shadows, literally and metaphorically.

"Well, fuck me, Richard," said a rumbling voice from beyond the tomb. Torchlight illuminated us as Ayer and Liman walked out from the shadows. "Looks like they didn't chicken out after all."

Chapter 37

Ayer carried a torch in one hand. The other was empty.

Liman carried a shotgun. The same one he'd had in my office? Displayed it prominently so we'd get the message: he wasn't here to be messed about.

Or maybe he was trying for another message.

Robertson said, "That's my bloody grouse gun."

"We couldn't go to your gaff and come away empty-handed," said Liman.

"Wouldn't be right," agreed Ayer.

I watched Robertson for a reaction.

He gave them nothing.

They'd burned his house down, fucked up his life. They had destroyed every hope Robertson had that his brother turned out right.

And he stood there, as they threatened him with his own gun, with his head bowed, deflated.

But then, could I really understand him?

Had I simply been projecting my own motives onto him?

Expecting him to be angry because I was.

Because I blamed these bastards for everything that had happened to me and to those around me.

If I closed my eyes, I could see Bill's bed in the hospital.

Blood stains on a polished wood floor.

Katrina Egg's sightless eyes.

The back of her head blown open: brains and blood and broken bone.

These Cockney pricks were responsible for all of that and more. And I now had a chance to pay back the pain that they had caused.

Burns had seen through me in the hospital. I wanted a fight, right enough.

Liman said to Robertson, "That the money?"

Robertson stepped forward, offered the case to Ayer.

The gentle rush of traffic on Riverside drifted lazily up to this remote place; we were not quite so isolated as we might have believed.

Ayer took the case from Robertson, yanking it roughly from the other man's grasp. Robertson stumbled back, his hands held up in supplication, as though afraid Ayer would attack him.

Liman adjusted the shotgun's position. A reminder. A warning. I made a show of noticing the gesture, keeping my own hands in plain sight to reassure the bald psychopath that I wasn't about to try anything stupid. He was close enough that the gun could do real damage. If someone could pick off a grouse at thirty yards, what could be done to me at two or three?

The wind picked up. My coat ruffled. The weight of the handgun bumped against my hip.

Just shoot the bastards.

All other sounds muted behind my own heartbeat.

Robertson took a step forward. "It's all there."

Almost cocky. A far cry from the man I had seen on the other side of the bridge.

Schizophrenic. Unpredictable. Robertson was beginning to worry me more than the Cockney hard men who I knew would shoot me in the head without a moment's hesitation.

Ayer smiled. Turned his back to us. Placed the briefcase on top of a nearby headstone.

Liman made sure Robertson remembered the shotgun, holding it aloft and waving it in the farmer's eyeline. Robertson noticed, but his attention was focused on the other man.

Ayer said, "The combination?"

Robertson recited three numbers, stumbling over them. Sounding jittery. He stuck his hands deep in his pockets. Looked like he was bracing himself against the cold of the evening.

Ayer clicked the locks. Robertson took another step forward, his hands still in his pockets.

"Just stay fuckin' still," said Liman. Not even bothering to raise the shotgun this time. His point already made. If we were too stupid not to have noticed, then that was our own fault. We were just two savages from a foreign country. Why should he care whether or not we were stupid enough to get out heads blown off?

Rain fell, spotting gently from the sky.

Thunder rumbled.

I watched Robertson closely. His expression, his stance and his attitude appeared strange and unnatural. I told myself it was nerves. The adrenaline coursing through his system.

Robertson took another step, right up close to Liman. The farmer wasn't exactly a tall man, but he towered over the bald Cockney.

Liman said, "I told you to stay fuckin' still."

Robertson's hand came out his pocket. Something flashed silver.

I tried to move, but my feet were stuck to the spot. Rooted like the headstones in the Necropolis.

Robertson made to stab Liman in the chest. Threw his weight at him, and his feet slipped on the muddy ground. He fell, off balance, and his arms flailed.

Liman was caught by surprise. He tried to swing the shotgun round and blow the farmer's brains out.

The twin explosions reverberated through the night.

And missed. The shot too wild to be accurate.

Robertson came in the inside of Liman's gun arm, his arms flailing as he struggled to regain his balance on the wet ground. The knife slashed out, missing its intended target and slashing the bald Cockney hard man across the cheek instead of slipping deep into his chest.

Ayer, startled by the shotgun's explosion, had spun round, knocked the half-opened case from the headstone.

The notes billowed out, caught in the gentle breeze and scattered in the air. They looked like dead leaves fallen from the canopy of trees above.

Robertson screamed.

Not with fear.

With anger.

The storm that had been threatening exploded around us, the rain falling hard and heavy.

A sound like horses' hooves clattered somewhere in the distance.

Chapter 38

Liman's face was sliced across his cheek, the open wound bleeding hard. The shotgun had fallen from his grasp. It lay maybe half a foot away from him.

Ayer looked surprised, hesitating for a moment when he saw what had happened.

Robertson tried to rush him. But the farmer was too slow, and Ayer was a man used to violence. The Cockney bastard grabbed Robertson's wrist and twisted. Robertson squealed. Tried to keep a grip on the knife.

I forced myself to lurch forward, made it as far as Liman. The bastard had one hand up at his face and was reaching out blindly with the other.

Trying to find the shotgun.

I kicked Liman hard. Caught him somewhere around the kidneys. He collapsed to his knees, his body jerking like in an epileptic fit.

I could only hope.

Ayer twisted Robertson's wrist hard. Robertson finally dropped the knife. The interruption of the shotgun blast had clearly shocked him back into a more sober state of mind.

The Cockney gave the fat farmer a second to realise what was happening before kneeing him in the stomach. Robertson slipped face first into the mud.

Liman was moaning. Rolled into the foetal position, hands gripping his face as though to stop the flow of blood where Robertson's blade had sliced deep.

I pulled Burns's gift out from my coat. Wearing the gloves, my fingers felt fat and clumsy. My balance wobbled and I felt my leg begin to seize up. Another thing to blame on the cold, perhaps. Or the exertion. It didn't matter. Any weakness could get me killed.

I found my feet again, putting as much weight as I could on my good leg, hoping it would be enough to keep me upright.

I held the handgun straight out in front of me. Locked my index finger through the trigger guard. Fought to keep my arms steady.

My muscles twitched uncontrollably.

The rain battered. Soaked my clothes, got in my eyes. I blinked hard to stop my vision from blurring. Bad enough the only light came from the moon and the torch that Ayer had brought with him.

Ayer looked at me with an expression that could have been surprise. "Fuckin' cunts!" he rumbled, before reaching inside his jacket and pulling out a gun. Likely, the same gun that had killed Kat. That had blasted a hole in Bill's stomach. That had killed so many people whose names and faces I would never know.

My trigger finger twitched.

But I didn't fire.

I couldn't.

Robertson had recovered his senses. He rolled away from Ayer, clambering clumsily to his feet. He was caked in mud, plastered with the rain-soaked cash that had been scattered from the briefcase. Before, he had seemed like a wild animal; a man with nothing to lose. Now, all of that anger had gone. His eyes were those of a man who had just woken from a nightmare.

Ayer turned his gun on Robertson. I was no longer a threat. I hadn't pulled the trigger a minute ago. Why would I have the balls to do it now?

Robertson was back on his feet. He took two steps away from the man with the gun.

"You killed my brother."

"He killed himself, the cunt."

"Put the fucking gun down!" I yelled, stepping forward. Holding out my own weapon to show I meant business. I still couldn't pull back on the trigger, hoped maybe I could fool Ayer into thinking otherwise. But he didn't even look at me.

Liman was on his knees, his left hand pressed hard against his bloodied face. The fallen torch shone directly on him. Blood, thinned out by the rain, caked his skin. He said, in a muffled voice, "Mathew, cunt's fucking serious and all."

Ayer turned his attention back to me. Swinging his gun away from Robertson.

The farmer took the opportunity; turned and bolted. At least, he staggered quickly.

Ayer made to turn.

I said, "Don't fucking think about it."

Robertson became lost in the shadows.

Ayer and I stood with our weapons trained on each other; two cowboys in an old spaghetti western.

Liman finally managed to climb to his feet. He

leant on an old gravestone for support, keeping one hand tight against his wound to stem the flow of blood. Robertson had cut him deep. The slash ran from just below his ear to maybe a quarter of an inch from his lips.

"Y'alright?" Ayer asked his friend. Eyes flicking past me, even if only for a moment. A second of concern, perhaps. Something approaching human in this monstrous bastard.

"Yeah," said Liman. "What a fuckin' waste of money." Looking around at the scattered cash; now soaked and ripped by the rainfall. He shook his head, and stepped forward.

I should have shot him right then. Showed these bastards I meant business.

But he was right. All of this was a fucking waste. Robertson had brought the cash. Christ, if he'd wanted them dead, why not swap the cash for a ringer? Why bring it here?

But I knew there were many things about my client I had failed to understand. If I stopped to consider them now, I would be a dead man.

Ayer looked at me. "Looks like your friend's fuckin' bailed on you."

I nodded. "Aye, sure. But he's not my friend. Just a client. I didn't know he was planning to cheat you. The only reason I came here was to protect his interests."

"Likely fuckin' story, eh?" said Ayer. His lips twisted. He showed teeth. Maybe he couldn't see the fear in my face yet, but he was willing to wait it out. "Shoulda fuckin' known he'd be a sneaky cunt like his brother."

Liman was holding the shotgun now. How did I miss that? He said, "This cunt's mine."

Ayer nodded, stepping backwards graciously. The two of them behaving like gentlemen.

Liman took another step forward. "Shotguns are pretty fucking useless. Clip a grouse from a distance, sure. But a man... you gotta be fucking close. And, then... even money whether he dies or just gets fucked up." He took a breath, let it out and squeezed the trigger.

Nothing happened.

The other problem with the shotgun: two triggers, two barrels, two shots. Liman had wasted his earlier during the struggle with Robertson.

I kept my own gun trained on Ayer. Watched Liman out of the corner of my eye. "Try anything and I'll shoot your fucking friend here." Brave talk, but I knew I was fucked. All I could do was wait and hope that someone down on Dunkeld Place had heard the shots and been savvy enough to call the police. Because I didn't know how much longer any of us could wait this out.

Ayer was the one who broke the standoff. He'd seen me for what I was, knew I didn't have the balls to pull the trigger.

He didn't want to talk. Or negotiate. Didn't really care whether I fired my weapon or not.

He smiled and let his arms drop to his sides. His own gun pointed harmlessly towards the sodden ground of the graveyard. I saw a gleam in his eyes. Pleasure. The sick bastard getting off on the idea that he was about to kill a man.

His eyes locked mine in a silent challenge.

There was one certainty: If I didn't shoot him, he'd kill me.

I'd thought if I could hold myself together for long enough, everything would work out. Now, I knew that was so much watered-down shite.

"I see you," he said, grinning like a wolf. This was a game to him.

I had no choice. I pulled back on the trigger.

Got nothing but resistance.

The safety still on.

Fuck.

Ayer laughed, raised his own weapon again. He'd had his fun. Had he known all along that even if I wanted to I couldn't have shot him?

I lashed out with my left fist, caught Ayer across the jaw. He stumbled back, more from surprise than pain; the punch had no real power behind it. A reflex. Fear and desperation guiding me now.

I fumbled with the gun. Trying to flick the safety to "off". The rain and the numbness of my fingers made it hard to feel details. I panicked, feeling the gun start to slip from my grip.

Out of the corner of my eye I saw Liman moving. The shotgun was useless as a firearm, but he could still swing it like a baseball bat, aiming for my head.

I ducked, falling on my arse in the mud. I crawled backwards, finding it hard with no grip on the ground. I was on my back, watching him as he raised the shotgun high, holding it by the barrel and using the stock like an axe-head. He meant to cave my skull in.

I was still struggling to flick the switch. Finally, it clicked and I aimed the gun high. Forced my finger into the trigger guard.

All it took was the smallest movement. The gun jerked in my hand. The explosion sent reverbera- tions up my arm, the pain culminating at my shoulder. Powder burned my face.

The bullet caught Liman in the chest. He stopped,

stood still for a moment, and then jerked once before falling backwards, collapsing onto the wet ground: an abandoned doll. Except no child would want a toy that looked like that.

Maybe my earlier attack had thrown Ayer off stride, but it hadn't put him down. He'd recovered fast and now his own gun was up and aimed at my head.

No need for words. I'd shot his mate.

No more games.

I moved fast, scrambling to my feet, ducking left, pushing past Ayer and making for the cover that lay deep in the heart of the Necropolis.

I felt the air catch fire somewhere beside my right ear. Didn't think about it, how close the bullet was. I just ran. Making for the nearby tangle of bushes. I dived through them. Scrambled for a tomb just beyond. Found it locked with no way inside. Pausing for a moment, I realised that there was only one entrance. Hiding inside would have been suicide. I still had my wits about me, at least.

I took a breather, leaned back against the stone walls of the tomb. A few seconds to orientate myself once again. Taking the weight off my legs, I realised that I had been running normally, the limp and the pain gone. Adrenaline?

My eyes were only just beginning to adjust to the light now that I was out of the sorry cover of trees. Above, the moon shone bright and full.

I listened to the sounds of the night, tried to quiet my heartbeat which threatened to echo into the shadows and reveal my hiding place.

I couldn't hear anything. But I knew I couldn't stay still for long. Ayer would figure out where I was, if he hadn't already. He moved softly for such a big man. Could easily have been one of the dead, himself.

I was on the south side of the Necropolis. Ideally, I should have made a beeline to the north, followed the direction Robertson had taken. Going south would take me out of the Necropolis, towards the new Balgay Cemetery. Lots of wide open spaces between gravestones that were no taller than knee height. Ayer would gun me down.

That way, I was a dead man.

I took a deep breath. The cold air burned my lungs. I turned towards the thick bushes and large, crumbling gravestones to the north. If I stayed in cover, I stood a chance.

And I realised, with a perverse joy, that I wanted to make it out alive.

I had come here intent on an odd kind of suicide, hardly caring if I lived or died and fully expecting that I would be killed by these Cockney psychopaths.

It was an odd revelation to have in a graveyard in the dead of night. Odd enough that I laughed out loud.

That was when Ayer came round the north side of the tomb. The light from his torch like a fist in the face.

Purple spots obscured my vision.

I backed away, holding up the gun, tripped over a root.

There was an explosion. Whether it was from my gun or Ayer's, I didn't know.

I slammed into the ground.

The mud oozed between my fingers. Stones ripped through the leather of my gloves and into the skin of my hands.

I gripped my gun tight, fought to keep a hold of it.

Something gave way in the back of my leg. In my

head, I heard what I thought was the sound of a muscle tearing. The leg flopped, uselessly. A white-hot burning sensation screamed across my thigh.

I was on the curve, right where the ground started to gently move to an incline at the southern face of the hill. I rolled with it, let gravity take over. Skidded part of the way, hit the slopes that led into Balgay.

The headstones became regimented. Materials became uniform; marble, mostly. The headstones were laid out in rows, each one exact and precise. Order rather than the chaos that prevailed in the heart of the Necropolis.

I had to keep moving. Tried to stand. The white fire in the back of my leg burned fiercely, and I fell to my knees, grabbing at a headstone for support. No such luck. I slipped into the mud. Wishing it would pull me under, let me rest at last.

I rolled onto my back, rested my head against the tombstone. Beaten.

Fucked.

He ran down to me. I could have shot him, but I couldn't find the strength to lift my gun.

Ayer smashed the heel of his boot against the back of my hand.

I screamed, but the noise was muted by the sound of the rain.

He did it again. All his weight smashing down. Bones cracked. I let go of my gun.

He kicked it away, out of reach. I saw it slip across the muddy ground.

Ayer stomped on my hand once more. The pain was less now, as though the repetition had somehow numbed me.

His foot didn't come down a fourth time. The hand was broken, I knew. Useless.

I thought: *this is it.*

Prepared. Accepting. Ready.

Ayer shook his head to get the rain out of his eyes.

And I remembered, just, that moment of revelation earlier. When I realised that I wanted to live.

I kicked out with my right foot. Caught his knee. He yelled and instinctively pulled on the trigger.

I closed my eyes.

Another explosion.

Something sharp cut into my face just below the left eye.

In the aftermath of the gunshot, the world went quiet, every sound muted.

The left side of my face stung. Rain sluiced into the open wound. My eye refused to open properly.

I kicked again. Thought I caught him in the head. Reached up, pushed myself forward using the headstone as leverage. Opened my eyes. Saw him on his knees. His gun was on the ground beside him. His hands grasped at his right foot.

And I realised what had happened. Any other situation, it might have been worth a laugh, a man like Ayer shooting himself in the foot.

I threw myself at the bastard.

Feeling the numbness in my left leg. At least it was moving again.

When I slammed into him, he fought back. Made to get up and roared with pain as he put weight on his shattered foot. I fell with him, landed on top. Gripped his right hand with my left in case he tried to reach for the gun he'd dropped. I lifted my head, and looked him in the eye. He attempted what I suppose was a cocky grin, but only ended up looking desperate. His left hand reached up and clawed at my face. I pulled away. Fingers pawed at the open wound below my eye. I tilted my head, pulling back from the reach of his fingers, and then brought it forward again. Dropping fast; smashing the bridge of his nose with the hard bone of my forehead.

The impact was dull and the crack of bones breaking was the clearest noise I had heard since the gunshot. His body went limp. I rolled away, lay in the mud struggling to take a breath.

Ayer moaned.

I reached out with my left hand and grabbed his gun, took a deep breath, and then tried to climb to my feet. Off balance, with my stomach churning and my vision blurred, I managed to stand. It took a supreme effort.

The rain battered down on my head.

Sirens wailed on the other side of the hill.

But for the moment, it was just the two of us. Here in the rain. In the darkness.

And I thought, *this time.*

I could kill him.

It would be easy.

Chapter 39

I looked down the gun at Ayer and in that moment I knew he'd been wrong about me. I could pull back the trigger, feel the kick, watch him die. There was nothing easier.

I was aware, now, of the coppers in the graveyard. Some concerned citizen had made that call. But I had to wonder if it was too late.

My left hand, holding Ayer's gun, started to tremble.

Ayer's eyes regained focus. He looked at me and smiled: the message clear enough. *Do it, then, if you've got the fucking bottle.*

And he really was laughing, a lunatic corpse, blood and mud caking his skin, eyes reflecting the moon.

I slipped my finger round the trigger. Locked my eyes on his, saw him encouraging me to go ahead.

"Put the gun down."

The wind brushed against the back of my neck. Cold but gentle.

I kept my eyes locked on Ayer's. The challenge was still there.

I kicked him in the face. I heard a crack as my foot impacted his already broken nose. I kicked him again. In the kidneys. I kept kicking him, made sure it hurt, made sure he understood.

A voice said, "Steed, leave him alone!" The same voice that had asked me to put down the gun.

I didn't listen.

"Leave him alone."

I looked up; Susan stood maybe three metres away. She held out her hand, palms flat to show she meant no harm. "It's over," she said. "Leave him to us."

I stepped back.

The other coppers were on me almost immediately, pinning my arms behind my back, trying to get me to calm down. Susan spoke to me, but her words were indistinct.

They cuffed me.

I raised my head to look at the headstone. Saw the damage where the stray bullet had shattered the marble. The sharp objects I'd felt tear open my face had been shrapnel.

The cops were talking, trying to make sure I understood I was being detained. I listened to them, allowed them to do their job. I was past giving a shite.

As they led me down to the vans, I turned my head and looked at the stone. I expected to feel sadness, maybe even anger. But instead I felt a kind of peace.

We passed one particular grave on the way and I said, hoarsely, "Stop."

No one listened.

"Stop. Please."

Susan heard me. She dismissed my escort, slipped her hand round my upper arm in case I tried to make a break for it. Copper's instinct.

She looked at the grave and said, "Jesus, McNee," and I wasn't sure if her tone was piteous or exasperated.

She shone a torch on the stone:

ELAINE BARROW
BELOVED DAUGHTER,
DEAR SISTER, DEVOTED FIANCÉE
1978-2007
NOTRE NATURE EST
DANS LE MOUVEMENT;
LE REPOS ENTIER EST LA MORT.

I thought about the wind on my neck earlier.

Remembered how her lips used to feel against my skin.

My legs gave way beneath me.

Chapter 40

It was seven in the morning by the time they got me to the station and set up in interview one.

My left eye was still half closed and beneath it the skin was swollen and bruised. But it was nothing serious. They'd cleaned out the wound, told me I'd just have to give it time. There was a good possibility I'd be marked for life. I'd joked with the attending doctors that a scar would give me character. Inside, however, I wasn't even close to smiling.

They did what they could with my hand. Broken metacarpals, joints fucked in the fingers and possibly a fractured carpal. The doctor had laid it all out for me. Told me he couldn't say for sure it would heal completely. For now it was a matter of wait and see.

Best case scenario was losing the use of my hand for several months. After that, if I was lucky, I might regain full movement. But for now it was bound up tight and God forbid I try and do anything with it until the doc instructed otherwise.

I asked him to look at my leg, told him I'd been having trouble with it recently. He carried out an examination without complaint, but said there was nothing wrong that he could see.

I thought about the psychiatrist.

The doctor told me what I needed was rest.

Not that I felt like doing much, anyway. With the painkillers they'd prescribed, I felt as though I could just float away. Although I was still dimly aware of a thumping discomfort that had no real localisation.

When they finally got me to the station, Lindsay brought a couple of coffees into interview one and somewhat grudgingly grabbed the seat across the table. Cordial, or as close as he could manage.

I took the plastic cup and nodded my thanks. He had his own personal mug decorated with a picture of a gull flying proud against a clear sky. The mug was scarred through use, the image beginning to fade.

I tasted the coffee. The liquid burned. When I swallowed, it hurt bad enough I wanted to scream.

Lindsay was straight down to business, not even bothering to ask how I felt. "These were the two men who killed Katrina Egg?"

"Aye."

"Under orders from Gordon Egg?"

I nodded. "Try getting Ayer to admit that."

Lindsay nodded. "When the doctors say he can talk, we'll be having a nice wee conversation." He looked me in the eyes, said, "You could have killed him."

"But I didn't."

He thought about that for a moment. Came to a conclusion: "Hardly worth a fucking victory dance."

We could have talked about Liman and Ayer. He could have asked me what David Burns had told me. But he didn't. After all, what use was I? A third-hand account of second-hand information would never stand up.

Nothing would ever connect the violence up at the Necropolis to Gordon Egg except rumours and hearsay. The coppers would get nothing on the big man. Mathew Ayer wasn't going to break down, even taking into account the death of his friend.

"You'd better pray that prick doesn't contradict what you've got to say for yourself." Talking about Ayer. An idle threat, of course. Nothing behind it. No enthusiasm even.

Lindsay sat back in his chair. His limbs flopped. The top buttons on his shirt were undone and his tie was loose. I wasn't under arrest. I'd merely been detained. Unless I gave him a good reason, I was gone in a few hours. Without charges, Scottish coppers can only detain a suspect for six hours barring requests for extension. He'd keep me in for the full six. Consider it some kind of payback.

All the same, he had to say something, make it look good. "One thing I still don't get: you just happened to be there? What, you stumbled across them taking a midnight walk through the Necropolis?"

I shook my head. Told the story again.

He waited, even though he wasn't really listening. He just wanted to piss me off, wear me down. When I was done, he said, "You didn't think to come forward? Through all the intimidation, all the threats, all the shit you knew a man like you shouldn't be handling, you just didn't think that maybe the professionals could have helped you? I mean, if you were an ordinary bloke on the street, maybe I'd understand. But you were a trained copper. What, since you became a citizen again you just turned off your brain?"

I stayed quiet. Didn't mention that I'd tried to talk to him earlier.

"Once in a while, McNee, I like to be disappointed. I like it when some cocky eejit turns around and surprises me. Does the right thing for once. I guess you don't have it in you to disappoint, eh? We could have caught these bastards, done it right. By the fucking book. No deaths, no unnecessary violence. We could have prevented your client from placing himself in danger. Now he's no longer the victim. Thanks to you, he's as much a criminal under the eyes of the law as those two Cockney bastards."

Did I say I thought he might have a point?

But nothing could have stopped Robertson. He'd been on the path before he stepped in my office. I gave him a direct line to the people he could blame for his brother's death. If he hadn't found me, then it would have been someone else. He'd been seeking revenge. He wasn't a killer. But he wanted to be. Gone over the edge long before I got involved.

"Anything you want to tell me?"

I shook my head.

"Maybe why your wee prick of a client thought it was a good idea to try and stick a knife in a couple of hard bastards who wouldn't think twice about snapping him in half?"

I sipped at the coffee, slowly. "No idea," I said. "But grief'll do funny things to a person."

Lindsay digested this. Considered it. Ignored it.

"Tell me something," I said. "You showed up mighty bloody quick."

"Like the cavalry, aye?"

"Sure. You were following me?"

"You were under surveillance."

My heart jumped. I thought about the gun I'd

taken with me to the meeting. How I'd told Lindsay I'd taken it from Liman, thinking it was a detail Ayer wasn't really going to dispute. Not when he had other matters to consider.

"How long?"

"Long enough."

I nodded.

"One more thing," he said, and if I didn't know him better I could have sworn he was doing some half-baked Columbo impression. "There was a third gun."

"Aye?"

"I mean, we've got the one you were pointing at the Cockney prick's head when we came in. And the shotgun his wee friend had been carrying. And then this third gun that comes from nowhere..."

"So... the prick had a backup weapon."

He smiled at that. "A backup weapon? Do you spend your days watching fucking American police shows?" He snorted. "A fucking backup weapon." The unasked question: *If that's true, how did you get hold of it?*

I shrugged, trying for nonchalant.

He didn't mention it again.

We sat there in silence for a while. It was the kind of quiet you find among old friends. Neither of us showing discomfort with it.

Chapter 41

Lindsay had wanted to make me responsible for the bloodbath at the cemetery. But I was nothing more than a bystander. The only reliable witness he had. He may have kept me in interview one for the full six hours, but that was more out of petty revenge than any real suspicion.

I was still worried about the gun.

I knew why Lindsay had mentioned it. Even if he had no proof that I had been in possession of an illegal firearm, he wanted to make me sweat.

Mission accomplished.

Susan was waiting for me when I left the station. Out of uniform. The harsh yellow light of the early evening sun seemed to soften when it fell on her.

In the car, I lolled in the passenger seat, watched the city roll past outside. In the aftermath of the storm, everything seemed quiet. The streets were almost empty, the glistening pavements reflecting the light from above. The walls of buildings were darkened with the rain, and the windows of parked cars were beaded with tiny droplets of water.

My body became heavy. The movement of the car and the peace of the city was enough to lull me towards sleep. After all, I thought, I deserved it. To close my eyes if only for a moment.

I barely remember arriving at the flat. I have only a vague memory of climbing the stairs, my arm around Susan's shoulders.

What I do remember is being in the living room, sprawled out on the sofa, Susan asking how I was doing.

And then: "Would you have killed him?"

"What?"

"Would you have killed him?"

"I wanted to."

"Is that really an answer?"

"No."

It was strange to hear myself talking. The painkillers were having their effect and I felt like an observer of my own life, surprised by my actions as much as anyone else was.

After Susan left, I went to bed, but stopped short of climbing in and collapsed on top of the covers. I didn't sleep. But I didn't want to move.

Except…

People thrive on closure, on the illusion of order in a chaotic world. I'm no different.

Loose ends make me uncomfortable.

Like James Robertson.

My client.

He had attacked two hard men. Killers. So full of primal rage, he'd taken everyone by surprise.

I knew that he was a changeable man. Had a temper. I'd witnessed his judgemental attitude towards other people, even his own family. But there was a great deal about him that I don't think I ever understood.

A great deal I'd seen and simply ignored.

If I hadn't become distracted by other events, I might have been able to help him. All of this could have been avoided.

I was missing a connection. Something had made him attack two men whose business, whose very nature, was death. Was it out of character? Or merely some part of my client I had blinded myself to?

What had I said to Lindsay in the interview room? Words slipping casually from my lips in the manner of a well-worn platitude: "Grief'll do funny things to a person."

And I wondered whether the grieving process had started for Robertson on the discovery of his brother's corpse, or if it had begun some time before even that.

***

I was pulled from sleep by my mobile ringing. Hadn't even thought about turning it off. Who was I expecting to call?

I answered; groggy.

Robertson said, "I killed him."

Sleep and painkillers made me slow. "What?"

He said it again.

When I didn't answer, he told me where he was. Said he wanted to talk.

***

Driving over the road bridge, I kept the window wound down. The wind blew hard into my face and kept me awake.

With my busted right hand, I found it difficult to control the car. Changing gears was the worst, letting go of the wheel and leaning my right forearm forward to try and keep it straight.

I should have stayed at home. Called Lindsay, told him what I knew.

I could claim that I wasn't thinking straight. That adrenaline, anger and painkillers were what kept me from picking up the phone.

But that was a load of shite. Because what stopped me from picking up the phone was the need to see this through to the end. The same stupid pride that had led me to kill a man.

The same stupid pride that convinced me I was the only one who could tie up the loose ends, set the world right.

Maybe I was already too late. Maybe I had the whole situation wrong.

I thought that I understood what Robertson was thinking. Finally knew why he had walked into my office that day. He had been looking for someone to blame for his brother's death. That was why he had come to me. A private investigator wouldn't step on his toes.

I should have seen all of this straight away, but for some reason I'd chosen to ignore it. Perhaps because something in his desire for revenge mirrored my own needs.

At St Michaels, I almost ramped up onto the embankment, as I turned onto the old farm roads. The car rumbled on uneven surfaces. Eventually, I came across an abandoned Mitsubishi Shogun, mud spattered across its tyre arches and the windows in need of a wipe-down. I parked behind the other vehicle, climbed out the car and slipped through the undergrowth.

James Robertson stood beneath the skeletal tree where his brother's life had ended. At his feet, a length of rope was coiled like a sleeping snake. The man's back was to me, and he stood perfectly still.

My feet cracked dead leaves and he turned. The movement near shocking, as though a statue had unexpectedly come to life. The whites of his eyes were red-raw roadmaps. He'd been crying.

I stepped forward.

"I think I get it now," I said. "The truth, I mean."

He stood his ground, his body language challenging me.

"You made him kill himself," I said. "That was why it looked so convincing. Did you plan that? I mean, was that how you thought you would avoid complicity? Was that how you avoided feeling like you had nothing to do with his death? Was that what made you think you weren't really a killer?"

"No."

"Then why?"

"He had to understand."

I nodded. "Make me understand," I said.

He hesitated. Then he told me everything.

Chapter 42

Robertson's living room the afternoon his brother came home:

"I want you to have it," Daniel said. "All of it. The money."

"And if I don't?"

Daniel shrugged, like it was no big deal, like people got offered cases of cash in their front rooms every day. "Then get rid of it."

That had been where Robertson's story ended the first time he told it to me. Daniel had walked out. Either upset by his brother's refusal to accept the proffered gift or so ashamed of his life that he couldn't stand to face judgement from all that remained of his family.

I should have picked up on the lie. Robertson's version begged the question of how he knew where to find the money when we agreed to meet Ayer and Liman in the graveyard. Begged a lot more than that. Had I deliberately blinkered myself to the holes in his story because, on some level, I connected with what I saw as a man in mourning?

In the shadow of the tree where his brother's body had been found, he told me the truth.

"Why?" Robertson had asked.

Daniel snapped shut the case, took a deep breath. "I made a mistake. Fuck it, I made a lot of mistakes. Took a lot of stupid fuckin' risks. And now I'm going to have to pay for them."

"Where did the money come from?"

Daniel shook his head. "Can't say, won't say. Bloke like you wouldn't understand. Wouldn't get it. It's not important. It's not hot money. Not for the police, anyway. No one's gonna notice you spending it."

"But they'd notice you?"

"It's not the money that's marked."

Robertson thought about this. He said, "Aye, all right. Then do this for me: tell me the bloody truth. All these years, for what you've told me, you might as well have been in a coma. I'm your brother. Christ, I deserve better than that."

Daniel hesitated. For a moment Robertson thought he might turn and walk out the door. But instead he took a breath and told Robertson the whole story. Who he was, what he had become, the terrible things he had done not only to others but also to himself.

Robertson only half believed what he was hearing. His eyes were opened to another world; one he knew existed but had never properly accepted as real. Robertson had known something of what his brother told him through newspapers, TV shows and what he had read in books. The effect of realising that it was suddenly so close to his own life was devastating.

When Daniel finally finished, any connection between the two men was lost forever. People talk about how you can forgive your family anything. That evening James Robertson realised what a crock of crap family was.

He had wanted his brother to return for so long. What had finally come home was some twisted parody of the boy he had once known; a disgrace to their father, to their family.

"I could have murdered him," he told me. "I mean, for all that he'd done he deserved to die. Aye, Christ, I should have. But I'm no killer."

I had to wonder who he was trying to convince.

He had asked Daniel whether he intended to do anything about his life, whether the man felt any remorse for the terrible things he had done.

"I'm fucked," Daniel said. "There's nobody left." His eyes dropped to the floor. "After mum died, you know, I think I began to realise something. I never really grew up. When I took off like I did, I wasn't running away from them. I was running away from myself. I could never have been a farmer. Couldn't have lived the life you have. Too fuckin' different, yeah? I always was. I was looking to make a point when I went to London. That I was different from you and from them. I wasn't just some farmer boy who had nowhere to go in life. I was gonna be some-body." He moved to the fireplace, let his fingers reach out and touch a framed photo of their parents. In the photo they were a young couple standing in some field together. Their father's arms were wrapped around their mother's waist. Her hair was long and dark and her face was unlined. She looked radiant. There was nowhere else in the world she would rather have been. Their father was strong and proud, his eyes twinkling with a joy neither son could easily associate with the man he would become.

"And somewhere it all went tits up," said Daniel. "I didn't become somebody. At least not like I wanted. I became a criminal, a fuck-up. Told myself I was happy. Even believed it, too. Except that... when you wrote and told me about mum, it was like I could feel her dying. Like a part of her had been inside me and I knew when she was dead, because it crumbled to dust and blew away on the wind. I was empty inside."

He shook his head, blinked away tears. "I know I sound like a poof, but it's true, every fuckin' word. We all have to come home one day, right? I thought I'd missed my day and I could never come home again. Felt like a fuckin' failure. The things I've seen, the things I've done and what was it that finally fucked me up? Ink on paper. My mother, who I barely even remembered and it was still like some bastard stuck a knife in my guts and twisted."

He clenched his fists, his knuckles whitening with the pressure. "Nearly two fuckin' years it ate at me, and I thought I could ignore it. Because that's what hard bastards do, yeah? They ignore things like that. They're men. Real men, like Lee Marvin, John fuckin' Wayne. Ray Winstone. He's fuckin' right there, he's the daddy. Because that's what it takes. Emotions, all that shit, it's what gets in the way. Never get attached to nothing except the money and the respect. Fight to keep every inch of both of them. For two years this shit ate at my insides. Chewed at my gut. Made me think of the fuckin' cancer that killed our mum. I couldn't take it no more, picked up the blower. Called Dad. You sent me the number when he moved house. Hoping I'd call him, right? And I did. I had to. Tell him I was sorry our mum was dead and say I would cry for her, but I wouldn't give a shit when he died. It was fuckin' stupid, like I'd regressed. Should have left the cunt behind a long time ago. Thought I had, too, until I heard his voice on the other end of the line. A fuckin' empty shell. He'd been the bogey man for so many years, yeah? Everything that made me frightened and ashamed and suddenly he was such a disappointment."

"You called him?"

"Yeah." Daniel couldn't meet his brother's eyes, knew what the other man had realised and couldn't deny the truth.

"That was the night he killed himself, wasn't it?"

"I didn't mean for him to..."

"He didn't leave a note. We never knew what was going on his head. He left everyone to guess what had happened. Making me feel like the one who did something wrong. I hadn't been the good son after all because he wasn't able to open up to me, to tell me..." Robertson stopped talking, his stomach churning. His fist lashed out instinctively. Daniel staggered backwards, clutching at his face. His eyes were wide with shock.

Robertson remembered who his brother was and his anger became fear. He stepped back, shrinking into himself. For protection.

Daniel Robertson simply stood there. "Everything I am," he said, "it's all been about running away from him. From myself."

"So you came back to offer me this money, to make amends?"

Daniel nodded. He looked at the money. "It's yours if you want it," he said. "It can't make up for what I've done, but... It's not just that. I came back because I realised that I had to take responsibility sometime."

Except Robertson could see something else in his brother's eyes. "For all you've done," he said, the viciousness in his voice surprising him, "you might

226

as well just kill yourself."

Daniel pushed aside his jacket, took the knife from his waistband. A big blade, serrated edge. Wood-effect handle. The same weapon Robertson would finally bring with him to the graveyard. The one he would use to attack Liman and Ayer.

Robertson said, "Are you going to kill me?" His chest ached, like his heart had just stopped.

Daniel held out the knife, gripping the blade between his thumb and forefinger. "No," he said.

Robertson almost burst out laughing when he realised what his brother was asking.

"If you don't kill me, I'm dead. You don't just walk out on a life like mine. They won't let you do it. The kind of sadistic bastards who work for Mister Egg."

"Bastards like you?"

Daniel looked shaken by the accusation.

Robertson turned away from the offered blade. "No," he said. "If you have to do it, you're going to do it yourself. But you're going to understand, Daniel, why our father was disappointed in you. You're going to understand why he took his own life. The shame he felt because of you."

***

Robertson told me the story slowly. As he spoke, his stance became less confrontational. His shoulders dropped. His legs buckled. His skin paled. I thought he was ready to pass out.

I said, "He went with you, just like that?"

"We were still brothers," he said. "And I think despite everything, underneath all of that London hard man shite, he knew he'd done wrong."

I'd only known Daniel Robertson as nothing more

227

than some abstract personality built from second hand stories and official reports. But I believed every word his brother told me. There was a haunted, melancholy sincerity to Robertson's voice that no man could fake. If nothing else, Robertson believed utterly in what he was telling me.

***

Robertson made his brother drive. Barely a word passed between them except when Robertson gave directions.

Finally they came to a small kirk, hidden on a hillside behind a curtain of trees. Cold and alone, the stone building sat hidden in the shadows as though ashamed of itself.

It appeared alien in the dark. Their memories were of a warm and welcoming building bathed in the sunshine of childhood Sundays. It should have evoked thoughts of love, family and stability. And instead it reached into their hearts and squeezed hard.

When he had grown up, and formed his own family, Robertson found religion again. Making sure his wife and son attended church every week even though they were hardly enthusiastic, and he himself had stopped truly believing long ago. It wasn't belief that mattered, but the ritual. What church represented was a family life lost long ago.

They parked outside. Sat in the car, looking at the building before them and recalling a childhood together that seemed so dim and distant it was hard to think of it as any kind of solid reality.

"I'm glad he's not around," said Daniel, finally, speaking about their father. "To see me like this."

His voice was quiet, the Scots accent harder, as

though just being here had brought back something of who he used to be.

"You understand, then?"

"I think so."

"I could kill you," he said. "I should kill you. My own brother." Trying not to cry. But he was ashamed of the man Daniel had become. And he knew Daniel was ashamed, too.

"But you won't," said Daniel.

Robertson shook his head.

Tears leaked from the corners of Daniel's eyes. The moonlight reflected in the liquid streaks. Robertson thought his brother had never grown up at all. He saw Daniel still as the teenager unable to communicate with his family and unable to give expression to anything but rage and frustration.

***

Robertson looked to the blasted tree. Shuddered as the anger and the guilt welled up inside him. He hadn't killed his brother. At least, he hadn't acted in any physical sense. But he had been complicit in the man's death.

What kind of a person could watch their own brother die, no matter the kind of judgements they had made on him?

He turned back to me. "I'm the same," he said. "A killer. A murderer. If I'd left instead of him, nothing would have changed. Except he'd be the one standing here." He spoke slowly. His voice was hollow and his eyes were wide with revelation.

I took a step forward.

"No," I said. "We all make choices and..."

I understood the difference between us, then. He

was ruled absolutely by what he had done. There was no choice for James Robertson. Like he said, if he and Daniel had swapped places, nothing would have changed except the name of the man in front of me.

I had chosen to be ruled by my anger. Because it was easier. Because it was there and urgent and important and...

Because I'd always thought of Elaine as the calming influence in my life. And without her, I'd convinced myself that it was easier to give in to the anger and frustration and guilt than to actually carry on living.

What does an investigator do? He involves himself in other people's affairs. Slips into their lives and loses himself in them. Becomes obsessed with the case and when it is done he is nothing. This is why each client is important.

Even the ones like Robertson.

***

He had watched his brother climb the tree. In his mind he saw Daniel as a young boy, climbing in sunlight, laughing at some childhood joke that would fade with the onset of adulthood. He tried to tell himself that this was how he would remember Daniel. The revelations of who that boy had become would fade with time and soon all Robertson would be left with would be memories of laughter and a time when the sun shone every day.

It was a lie, and even then he knew it.

At church, when they were young, the minister had talked about character and strength and responsibility. This was something that had been instilled in James Robertson. Maybe he was predisposed to accept it. He would never know. He wasn't sure that he'd ever care to know, either. It wouldn't help him to understand why his brother had never taken the same lessons on board.

Daniel said, "I'm sorry," the soft words carried by the evening breeze.

There was no crack.

Daniel's neck should have snapped. Robertson had been expecting it. But the sound never came. When Robertson opened his eyes, he saw his brother twisting in the breeze. Daniel's legs kicked out, searching for a purchase they would never find. His hands reached up to grab the noose, tried to loosen its grip around his neck.

Robertson fell to his knees and closed his eyes so tight he thought blood would squeeze from between the lids. His brother made guttural, primal noises.

After what felt like hours, there was silence. Robertson couldn't say how long it really was. Could have been fifteen seconds. Could have been as many minutes.

Robertson stood up, kept his eyes on the dead leaves beneath his feet. He left the clearing, taking slow, deliberate steps.

In his mind he played and replayed the events as he would later report them. He even convinced himself that his version was the truth. He had played no part in his brother's death.

***

I could have collapsed and joined Robertson on the ground among the dead leaves and the dirt. But when I thought about him as he watched his brother die, the empathy within me vanished.

231

I turned to walk away.

"Wait."

I kept my back to Robertson, but I stopped walking.

"You have to understand. For what I did, for... for all of that... oh, Christ... I'm asking you..."

He didn't have to. I understood.

But I didn't care.

"Please!"

"Aye," I said. "You're right. You deserve to die."

But I thought it was a better punishment for him to live with what he had done.

Chapter 43

After I refused to help him die, Robertson tried it himself.

Tied a rope to the branch that had held his brother's corpse. Let himself fall.

But it didn't work. The tree refused to support him. The branch snapped before he was strangled. He landed wrong, damaged his spine. Might even have got his wish and died out there if he hadn't been found by a young couple walking their dog.

It still didn't feel like justice to me.

***

Susan kept me updated on Ayer's arrest. She came to the flat and we drank coffee together. The first time, she sat on the sofa the same way Elaine used to, with her legs curled up underneath her.

"Please," I said, nodding to an armchair opposite. "Sit over there."

She seemed to understand.

I should have taken time off. I was no use for physical work. I started using the crutches again, claiming a tear in my hamstring. Maybe I was right about that. My hand was useless for weeks. I attended physiotherapy and was given too many stern lectures.

I tried to lose myself in those cases I could still pursue.

***

The arrest incident at the Balgay Cemetery made the papers. Some mention was made of my involvement although the details were vague. It brought me a few new clients.

I took on enough to see me through.

***

Susan stopped by every second day. Sometimes at the flat, sometimes at the office. All we did was talk. Sometimes about what happened. Most of the time just about whatever was on our minds.

"It's nice," she said.

"What?"

"This. Hearing you talk. Like a human being."

I felt myself blush, although I wasn't sure why. "Sure."

"Aye, I mean it's nice that you're not turning away. Like you always do."

I thought about the morning after we slept together.

And then about when I confronted Elaine's father

in the interview room.

Andy in the A&E.

Bill in the hospital ward.

Each time, I'd expected them to understand. And each time, I'd failed to speak, the words drying up before they even reached my lips.

If I'd just said my piece, maybe things would have been easier.

***

Bill's recovery was protracted and painful. The odds were in his favour, perhaps, but every day was a new struggle. Physically and mentally.

During my visits we talked about everything except what had happened. What was there either of us could say?

***

I went back to Elaine's grave. Stood there for ten minutes and found I couldn't say a word.

I had so many things I wanted to tell her, but they could wait.

I had thought about asking Rachel to accompany me. But she had done more than enough. Some things, you have to do alone.

***

Ayer was stabbed in Perth prison. Left to bleed out in the showers. Medical staff couldn't get to him in time and he died that same day.

The killer was caught and said he didn't like the way Ayer spoke. Hell of a thing to be killed for, having an English accent.

But everyone knew that was only half the story.

The killer was a recidivist dealer who got caught too many times trying to sell pills to punters outside a Perth nightclub. He had no history of unprovoked violence and staff at the prison expressed their surprise at what he did.

What the papers didn't say was that the man had ties to David Burns.

Chapter 44

Susan had to drive me. My hand wasn't healing well. It wasn't safe for me to go out on the roads.

She said, if I did, she'd arrest me herself.

When we got close, I said, "Here," and she pulled over to the side of the road. I got out the car and she joined me as I clambered onto the stone wall. I struggled, trying not to use my fucked hand. Susan reached out to help me, but I pulled back.

We swung our legs over, faced away from the road. In the distance the gently rolling Lomond Hills rose to meet the horizon.

Susan said, "Why here?"

"This was where she died."

She didn't say anything.

"I was selfish," I said. "I wanted to hang on to whatever I had left of her. This place gave me something like that."

"It sounds morbid."

"It was," I said.

"And now," she said, "why come back?"

"I guess I needed to say goodbye to all this in some way."

"So why am I here?"

I hesitated, watched the hills for a moment. "Maybe I felt I couldn't do it alone."

Her lips turned upward in a gentle smile.

Gently she reached out, placed her hand on top of mine. Her fingertips brushed the bandages. She stayed like that for a moment before pulling back, swinging her legs over the wall.

"I'll be nearby."

I sat alone for a few minutes as she walked further down the road, looking at the hills in the distance.

I looked at the field which seemed so peaceful in the daylight.

I thought about what Rachel had said in the graveyard about moving on. I turned to look at Susan, who was lost in her own thoughts.

I took out my mobile. Dialled in a number I hadn't called for over a year.

When Martin Barrow answered the phone, I tried to speak, but all that came out was a croak.

"Who is this?" he asked.

Finally I said, "I didn't kill your daughter. I know you need someone to blame, but it's not me. And I know we should have said all this a long time ago, but... we need to talk."

And then I waited.

Acknowledgements

The quotation on Elaine's gravestone comes from Pascal's *Pensees*. Blame six years of studying philosophy at the University of Dundee.

Any errors in fact, procedure or history are mine. Most of them were made in the name of that old fiction writer's standby, *dramatic necessity*. Or at least that's the story I'm sticking to. Anything that's accurate, chalk it up to contributions from any one of the following:

Dot and Martin McLean: My parents. If I listed all the reasons why, we'd have to publish a whole other book.

Allan Guthrie: Who stepped in when everything was looking hopeless. Agent, friend, and demented genius.

Ross Bradshaw: For taking a chance on a debut crime novel and offering those final suggestions that helped smooth it all out: thank you.

Linda Landrigan; Jen Jordan; Gerald So; Kevin Burton Smith; Sarah Weinman; Jon Jordan; Ruth Jordan; Sandra Ruttan; Bryon Quertermous: All helped me develop my work in print and on the web.

Charlie Stella; Ray Banks; Adam Roberts; Martin McLean (again!): All took the time to read early drafts and point out the flaws, the idiocy and even the bits that worked.

Robert Simon MacDuff-Duncan; Steven Wicks; Jim Smith; Peter Heims: All answered questions over the last four years (some of them probably won't even remember) regarding police work, the differences between Scots and English law, and the life of the PI.

Rebecca Simpson; Gary and Kim Smith; Tim Stephen; Donna Moore; Dave White; Lesley Nimmo; Kevin Wignall; Steven Torres; Sean Chercover; The Gone-but-not-forgotten Blue and Red Shirts from the Bookworld days; my friends from Ottakars... and now Waterstones; anyone who feels I missed them out (there will be a few; I've got the memory of a goldfish): for moral support, the occasional kick in the arse, and many, many drinks to see me through long evenings. Thanks, guys.

And in memory of:

Issy Rose, 1953-2008